I0699148

BY MIDNIGHT

A THRILLER

BEYOND THE BRIDGE SERIES
BOOK 3

SUSAN SPECHT ORAM

SOS COMMUNICATIONS

This book is a work of fiction. Names, characters, businesses, organizations, events, and places other than those clearly in the public domain, are either a product of the author's imagination or are used fictitiously. Any semblance to actual persons, living or dead, events or locales is entirely coincidental.

BY MIDNIGHT Copyright © 2024 by Susan Specht Oram. All rights reserved. No part of this publication may be reproduced, stored in any retrieval system, or transmitted, in any form by any means, electronic, mechanical, photocopying, recording or otherwise, without prior written permission from the publisher except in the case of brief quotations embodied in critical articles and reviews.

NO AI TRAINING: Without in any way limiting the author's and publisher's exclusive rights under copyright, any use of this publication to "train" generative artificial intelligence (AI) technologies to generate text is expressly prohibited. The author reserves all rights to license uses of this work for generative AI training and development of machine learning language models.

Published by SOS Communications LLC in 2024

www.susanspechtoram.com

First Edition

ISBN: 979-8-9891982-7-6 (paperback)

ISBN: 979-8-9891982-6-9 (e-book)

✻ Created with Vellum

PREVIOUSLY

By Midnight is the third book in the *Beyond the Bridge* series and it can be read as a standalone.

The first book is *Under Jackson Bridge* and the second is *Missing Man*.

Previously:

When Irena and her friends set out on a boat trip, a rogue wave washed Irena and her ex-husband Jack overboard. Irena was pulled from the water, but Jack was missing and left behind clues to a secret life. He was later found in the hospital, but he has amnesia.

A LAST JOB

ELGIN JOHNSON

Wincing in pain, I grit my teeth and stare at my throbbing thigh. After doctors removed an arrow from my leg, I was wheeled down a hall and spotted Jack Fishbone in another room. He's the deadbeat I've been chasing, which led to me being shot by an arrow. I clench my fists and frown. I'm tired of chasing debtors down. My boss doesn't know it yet, but after I collect this cash, I'll quit this wretched job.

I swing my legs over the edge of the bed and stand, my knees shaking and sweat beading on my brow. Grabbing a pair of crutches, I shuffle ahead, taking tentative steps. Sharp pain from my right thigh makes me moan. I limp into the hall, thinking about how to make Fishbone pay his overdue debt.

1

BUZZ

My dog Happy whines as I pace in my office at the bookstore. Rain patters against the window pane. I ruffle my dog's ears and say, "Let's go for a walk to clear my mind."

I pull on my coat, hook Happy to the leash, and take him past the front desk. I say to my assistant, "Be back in a bit."

She smiles. "Going for a walk?"

"Yep, just a spin around the block."

I step outside on a gray morning. Happy trots beside me as we go through town. If I didn't have my dog with me, I'd go to Gigi's Café and have breakfast.

Walking along, I mutter to myself, "I pray Jack won't remember how he got hurt."

I'm not proud of my dark rage and flash of anger,

lashing out at Jack, my best friend, but when he wanted to take my girlfriend and their daughter away with him, I couldn't help myself.

IRENA

I steer my boat toward a vessel in distress, going to help a boater who ran out of fuel. A gray-haired woman and man stand on the stern with their arms crossed, wearing dark blue jackets. A strong breeze tugs at strands of her hair, pulled back in a bun. I come alongside and say, "Permission to come aboard?"

The woman, who looks to be in her seventies, says, "Yes."

I lash the boats together at midships and grab a jerrycan of diesel fuel. Rain wets my face as I step over the gap to their boat.

He scratches his whiskered chin and doesn't meet my eyes. "Are we glad to see you."

She glares at the man. "Thanks for coming on short notice for two old fools who didn't have the sense to check the fuel before leaving the dock."

I smile. They paid by credit card, but it's a good feeling to help another boater out.

The man frowns. "I was afraid we'd wash up on those rocks."

I glance at a rocky part of Cedar Island's shoreline and say, "You were getting pretty close. I'm glad you called a 'Mayday' when you did."

The skipper opens a metal cap in the deck and holds a funnel as I pour the fuel. When the can is empty, I say, "That'll get you to the fuel dock."

I say goodbye and board my boat, stowing the jerrycan and casting off. Putting the engine in gear, my boat pulls away. I turn the wheel and head south toward the marina.

Rain splatters on the windshield, and the wiper blades swish back and forth. Biting my lip, I mull over how Jack lost his memory. The doctors say he has a traumatic brain injury, but how did that happen? I turn into the marina, slow my speed and putter past a rocky breakwater.

I pull into the slip, secure the lines and hop off. Rain drizzles down, and mist rises from the pavement. Pulling up the hood of my raincoat, I wave to a friend in the marina office and hurry to the parking lot.

Hopping in my car, I head toward home. I drive by Buzz, who is walking his dog in the rain. I really need a cup of coffee. My stomach growls, and I pull over, parking by Gigi's Café. A scone, a slice of quiche, and hot coffee sounds like the right recipe for a dreary day.

As I climb out of the car, Buzz jogs over and says, "Want to grab breakfast together?"

His wide grin reminds me of better times. I swallow and say, "Sure, why not. I guess I could use the company."

He gestures to the dog. "Okay if Happy sits in your car while we eat?"

I cock my head. "I'm not a fan of wet dog smell, but the best dog in the world deserves a break from the rain."

I hold the car door open, and Happy hops inside. Buzz and I walk to the café's front door, where he stops and says, "After you."

I push the door open and wonder how this breakfast will go. My stomach sours when his arm brushes against mine. My mind calls for distance because he's a liar.

We sit at a vacant two-top in a room full of people we know. Jacklyn Stone, the former owner of the garden store, waves with a twinkle in her eyes from an adjacent table. She has on her trademark shorts and mismatched socks, despite the rainy weather. She has become a friend, and she's working on a housing development on the edge of town, so she's gone from a grieving widow to hopefully becoming a real estate mogul.

A woman in a pink workout gear wiggles her fingers at me, and I smile back. Her curly-haired table mate leans over, talking about a book. She says, "I knew what was going to happen early on. The twist at the end didn't surprise me at all."

The café owner, Karina, comes by carrying a coffee pot. She says, "Coffee?"

I groan. "Yes, please, and gallons of it. I've been out on the water, and it's before ten in the morning."

Buzz smiles. "And I've had two dog walks. How are you, Karina?"

She pours coffee and grins. Her nose piercing sparkles, reminding me of the engagement ring Buzz offered. I massage my temples, where a headache is starting.

Karina says, "The café is coming together. I bought a new dishwasher and a second frig. Mr. Frackus is helping me. And I unloaded my pottery kiln last night. The bowls are for sale if you're interested."

I say, "I'll take a look."

We order scones and quiche, and she moves to another table. Buzz leans over, looking me in the eye. "What are we doing, living apart? I can't imagine not having you in my life."

I blow out a breath, and I'm about to answer when the door opens. A breeze blows in, and Mike, the marina manager, looks around the room. He locks eyes with me and comes over, sliding a chair over to our table.

Buzz murmurs to me, "I hoped we'd have a moment alone."

I nod, and my head whirls from all that's happened, with Jack going missing and being found as a John Doe in the hospital. "We'll find time to talk, but it looks like it won't be this morning."

Mike adjusts his ball cap. Like many men in our town, he wears a flannel shirt with jeans, and his short gray hair and trimmed beard look like the city uniform. He sits and says, "I won't stay long, but how's Jack? I heard he lost his memory. Did he and Abby get hitched in the hospital?"

Buzz and I glance at each other and tilt our heads the same way, like we've done since we met in grade school. I say, "Jack looks awful, and Kelly thought he was a stranger at first. He had surgery last night, and it seems that he and Abby were married."

Buzz frowns. "He has amnesia. They're not sure if his memory will come back."

I clear my throat and say, "Jack didn't recognize Kelly and it's tearing her apart."

Mike claps a hand to his heart. "The poor kid. That's tough. Hope he remembers his own daughter soon."

Buzz nods. "It's really rough on her."

Gazing at Buzz, I recall why I fell in love with him. He's always been kind to my daughter Kelly and treats her with respect, but he has lied to me. He is always around, having been in our friend group that formed in high school, twenty-five years ago.

Mike stands. "Thanks for the update. I'll leave you to it."

ABBY

I call in sick and tell my boss, "I got married to the man I love last night, and I need a few weeks off. I hope you'll understand."

She shrieks, and I picture her bouncing up and down. Her shoulder-length blond hair will be covered in a hair net, as required by health and safety regulations. She says in a loud voice over the noise of manufacturing machines in the background, "Are you joking? Because if not, I'm beyond happy for you."

A wide smile spreads across my face. Jack is asleep in the hospital bed, so I stand by the window speaking in a low voice, which is the exact opposite of how I feel about my news. I say, "I can't believe it. I'm delirious with joy."

"Who is the lucky guy?"

"I've known him since high school and always had a crush on him."

My boss laughs. "High school was a long time ago."

I roll my eyes. "Thanks for the reminder. His name is Jack Fishbone, and he's the guy who went missing. He has a traumatic brain injury and needs time to recover in the hospital."

"Take as long as you need," she says. "We'll cover for you."

"It looks like I need to add him to my health care insurance."

"Stop by and sign the forms or go online. He's lucky he married you, Abs, for a million reasons."

My face heats at the compliment, and I glance at Jack, whose mouth is open while he sleeps. I whisper, "No, I'm the lucky one."

We hang up, and I pocket the phone, looking out over the town of Mt. Vernon from the hospital's eighth floor. Beyond two and three-story buildings, the river gleams, snaking its way through town.

Jack's eyes flick open, and I hurry over to him. "My boss gave me time off. But I was thinking about how Kelly's been hurt. We need to fix that. You could pretend to know her next time she visits."

He shrugs and winces, as if the movement caused him pain. "I don't want to fake it. Before I was rolled into the operating room, I vowed to be a better person. I can't pretend. I just don't remember her."

FRANKIE

I clamp my jaw shut and consider the disaster that landed in my lap. Standing up at my desk in the FBI's Seattle office, I say to Special Agent Brick, "We finally found Jack Fishbone, but it fell apart. We need to figure out how our key witness in the fraud trial lost his memory. Did criminals hit him in the head, so he wouldn't testify? Or was it an accident?"

He puts down a meatball sandwich, wiping his mouth on a napkin. The aroma of grilled onions, tomato sauce, and pork and ground beef meatballs wafts past. He says, "I'd put my money on the creep who broke into Jack's apartment. Remember how we spoke with him after they operated on his leg?"

I cross my arms. "Sure do. He pretended to be sound asleep, but kept opening his eyes a tiny bit and peeking out while we stood there."

"He may have knocked Jack out after trying to get him to cough up the cash for those high-end sneakers. And he went on a rampage at Jack's, wielding a baseball bat."

"It's a good theory. Let's shelve that for the time being and go over what we have from Jack before he went missing."

Brick says, "We've got recordings of interviews with him, and his signed statements. We'll dig into his laptop for anything that might help us."

I nod. "The ex-wife wants his laptop back when we're finished, so she can read his half-finished book on the history of jogging." I snicker. "How many people will want to read that?"

Brick smiles. "About twenty-three people in Eugene, where the Olympic time trials for track were held."

I tap a finger to my lips. "Irena wants his laptop, but now that Jack is found, and he's married, he might want it, or his new wife will. But whatever we do, we can't let that scum Craig, who ran the scam on older people, slip out of our hands on a technicality, or lack of evidence."

"We'll nail him."

KELLY

When my dad disappeared in a boating accident, I thought I'd never see him again. But Abby, my mom's best friend, found him at the hospital. He had short choppy hair and a bruised black eye, and he didn't recognize me. I ran to the bathroom and retched.

The doctors aren't sure if his memory will come back. Mom says we'll get through this, but all I know is it hurts. I want my dad back, the one I had before he went missing.

I walk to school and, with each footstep, I pray under my breath, "Make Dad's memory come back, so he'll know me."

2

IRENA

I'm practicing the violin, pulling the bow across the strings and wincing at the scratching sound, when Kelly comes home from school. She drops her backpack by the door and opens the fridge, pouring a glass of orange juice. "Hi, Mom."

I set down the violin and pull her into my arms, giving her a hug. "Let's go see your dad at the hospital today. Maybe he'll remember you this time."

She frowns, and I hold her as she weeps, shoulders shuddering. I murmur, "He'll get his memory back. It's just a matter of time."

When she pulls away, I say, "Do you want to invite Plum over after we see your dad? I can make gluten-free noodles for dinner."

"I can't face my friends and their questions right now."

I say, "We could order pizza? That'll make things better."

She rolls her eyes. "Dad not knowing who I am is a bigger problem than pizza will solve." She shuffles down the hall, closing her bedroom door, and I stare at it, hoping this isn't the beginning of teenage rebellion.

Taking the violin in my bedroom, I rub my temples. I must be strong to help her get through this heart-breaking time until Jack recognizes her. I prop open the blue student work book on a pillow and pick up the violin, tears streaming down my face as I play. I know what it feels like to be without a father, because when I was young, my dad was sent to prison for killing a man in a bar fight. My mom and I loaded the car and left. We drove for hours, ending our journey in Millersville by the water. My mom passed away, so I'm all that's left of our family to support Kelly.

As I slide the bow across the strings, a worrying thought comes to mind, and I furrow my brow. My dad was a mean-spirited man, and I haven't kept in touch. What if he is granted parole and he tries to find me? Blowing out a breath, I continue practicing. I don't have to worry about seeing him again. He's in for life.

JACK

Abby holds my hand while a doctor in a white lab coat talks to us.

Dr. Wang says, "The swelling in your brain has gone down, but it's too soon to predict when we will release you from the hospital."

I say, "I'm pretty weak, but I was hoping to get out of here today."

Abby smiles, squeezing my hand.

Dr. Wang says, "How is your pain level?"

A jab of pain hits me, and I suppress a groan. "My head really hurts."

"We'll get you something for the pain. You will need to be able to walk, eat, use the bathroom and have little to no pain before we discharge you."

I wince and put a hand to my forehead, where a splitting headache throbs.

When the doctor leaves, Abby says, "Hang in there, hubs. We'll get through this."

Stabbing pain pierces my skull, making me moan. I want to leave the hospital and go home to start a new life with my new wife. "I wish I remembered how I hit my head."

She scowls. "If someone did this to you, they deserve to die."

I try to crack a joke but it falls flat. "Oh, it's nothing, just a little traumatic brain injury." She frowns, and I say, "Seriously, I have to figure out happened to me. If only the pain would let up."

CRAIG

I clench my jaw and peer through metal bars. I'm being held in jail, but the trial hasn't been scheduled, and I can't make bail. Jack was in charge of the scam, and he should be locked up, not me. I'll never forgive my friend for ratting me out.

My roommate snores on the lower bunk while I plot sweet revenge on my friend. I wish I could find someone in prison to take out a hit on Jack, but I don't have the money to pay them because my assets are frozen. I could write threatening letters, but the guards would open them, and I'd be in more trouble. I want to find a way to hurt Jack and come out clean. While I wait behind bars, I have all the time in the world to plan ways to get back at him.

ABBY

I hold Jack's hand and listen to his doctor discuss his prognosis. My neck is sore from sleeping on the pull-out recliner on the first night of our honeymoon. The doctor leaves, and I say to Jack, "It doesn't matter where we are, at my place or in the hospital, if we're together. That's what matters most."

He gives me a thin smile and lets out a sigh. "I'm so glad you found me."

I nod, recalling how I tracked Jack down in the hospital with the help of a stranger on social media. Luck and perseverance led to us getting married. I say, "Come on, swing your legs over the edge of the bed. I'll help you walk a few steps. It's time you tried."

I pull over a metal walker and offer my hand to help him. His eyelids flicker. He whispers, "I'm not ready. Let me sleep a bit more."

He falls asleep in seconds, and I walk to the window, looking out. Love and long-held dreams of a life together are warring with the reality of marrying a wounded man with major gaps in his memory. My eyes fix on the winding river across town and hope I can be strong enough to face what comes next. I must be as mighty as a rushing river and as life-giving as the fertile farmlands beyond the bridge.

I glance back at Jack, giving him a half-smile. Perhaps we can give Kelly a half-sister or brother before the year is out.

3

KELLY

When the violin playing stops, I hurry from my room to knock on my mom's bedroom door. "Can we go see Dad now?"

She opens the door, and her cheeks are streaked with tears. "Sure, let me stop in the bathroom first." The violin rests on red velvet in the case on her bed. She snaps the case closed. "If you want, you can play violin too and take lessons."

"I'll stick with dance. Isn't it a bit late to take up playing at your age?"

She smiles. "Not to sound corny, but it's never too late to follow your dreams. I've always wanted to play violin, but my mom didn't have the money to rent one and pay for lessons. She gave me a kazoo for Christmas when I was nine instead."

I laugh. "That's a big difference, a kazoo instead of a violin."

"She tried her best, and that's all we can do." She steps to the bathroom. "I'll be right out. Will you text Abby and tell her we're on the way? I don't want to burst in and surprise them. It is their honeymoon, even if they're in the hospital."

I wrinkle my nose at the image of Dad kissing Abby. "Please don't mention the honeymoon again. I don't want that in my head."

She bites her lip. "What's weird is he seemed to know who Abby was, but not us. Why her?"

I shrug. "Maybe she was his secret girlfriend I was supposed to meet."

She starts to close the bathroom door and stops. "I would've known if she was his secret girlfriend. Your dad would've told me."

I tilt my head. "Except he didn't. You didn't know he was in debt, borrowing money from shady people."

She nods. "True. I didn't know he was an FBI informant."

I put a hand to my heart. "I hope he'll know me when I see him today."

"You're his daughter, and he won't forget who you are, but it might take time to get his memories back. Hold on, and I'll be right out." She closes the bathroom door, and I lean my forehead against the cool hallway wall. I'm invisible without my dad seeing me as a person related to him. When he didn't know me, I didn't feel real without his recognition. I'm a walking zombie of regret.

The toilet flushes, the faucet comes on and stops, and the bathroom door creaks open. "Hey there, sweet girl. What're you thinking about?" She wraps an arm around my shoulder, and I lean in. Her hand is damp.

I say, "If a daughter isn't known by a parent, do they cease to exist? Maybe I'm just a figment of your imagination."

She rubs my back. "Those are big thoughts. You're as real as they come, my love. You are my world, so you are special to me and everyone who cares about you."

I say in a choked-up voice, "No one cares about me."

She looks me in the eye. "Buzz does, Abby definitely does, even though she's busy now. You matter to us, and your dad forgetting who you are has nothing to do with how important you are. You are loved. You are important. And if my mother was here right now, she'd smother you in a big, ferocious hug."

I groan, pretending to push her away, but step into her embrace, smelling her sea-scented hair from working on the water.

She pats my back. "Let's go see your dad and, I can't believe I'm saying this, his new wife. These are weird times."

"Tell me about it."

On the way to the hospital, Mom turns on music, probably to put me in a better mood. I don't mention it, but I didn't text Abby to say we're coming to visit. I didn't want to give her a chance to tell us not to come.

4

———

IRENA

I drum my fingers on the steering wheel and drive to the hospital. My glance at Kelly, who is staring out the window. She needs her dad. I don't know what I'll do if Jack doesn't recognize his daughter today.

My throat tightens with tears, because Jack didn't know who I was, despite us being close and talking almost every day. A twinge of jealousy stabs me as I head for the hospital. He seemed to know Abby at first sight, but not me, his ex-wife, or his own daughter. I shake my head at how he married my best friend.

Kelly says, "Why are you shaking your head?"

I let out a breath. "I never expected your dad to get married again, especially to Abby. It feels weird."

She nods. "I guess I have a step-mother. It's probably better it's her and not someone else."

I say, "I wonder where they'll live when he gets out of

the hospital. Her studio apartment is small for two people. Can he hold down a job with his memory issues? He had trouble with that even before the accident."

Kelly says, "I think they have bigger issues on their minds than where they live and his getting a job. Can he even walk? He looked weak and not like Dad at all."

"He's not the same, that's for sure."

JACK

A nurse wearing yellow framed glasses and her hair in a ponytail comes in and says, "I'd like to get you walking and going to the bathroom."

I clear my throat. "Might as well give it a try."

I push a button, so the head of the bed goes up, and pull off the covers. I don't know how long I've been in the hospital, but my muscles are weak. I swing my legs over the edge and sit up.

A big hairy guy leans on a walker in the hall, staring in my room. Our eyes lock, and a shiver runs up my spine. I'm afraid of him, but I don't know why. I look away.

The nurse says, "Let's see if you can stand on your own."

My head throbs, making me wince, and I muster the strength to stand. The nurse holds my elbow for support.

My legs tremble, and I sit on the bed. Blowing out a breath, I say, "What a wimp. I can barely stand up."

"I'll get you a walker," she says. She leaves and brings back a metal walker, setting it in front of me. "Try it now, if you have the energy."

I take a breath and rise, gripping the walker, and taking small steps in my bright yellow hospital socks with non-slip treads. I'm shuffling like an old man, barely moving ahead. What a humbling journey this is on my road to recovery.

Abby breezes in the room with a wide smile, holding a cup of coffee. "Look at you, up and around. You'll be back to your old self in no time."

I nod and concentrate on getting to the bathroom door. I admire her optimism, but because I don't recall who I was, I don't know how to get back there and reclaim my old self. A sense of inner knowing taps inside. I might not like who I was before, and maybe I don't want to return to the old Jack Fishbone. I was deep in debt, Abby says, and I don't want to do that again. She hasn't told me what I spent money on, so I need to ask her.

I reach the bathroom door and rest a bit, leaning on the walker and puffing for breath. I thought maybe I had been a professional athlete, like a basketball player, but given my weakness, I doubt I was a pro star dunker. Maybe I was a beer and flip flop kind of guy. I'll focus on getting my strength back and leaving the hospital. When

I'm living with Abby, I'll have time to get to know who I was and who I want to be. Would I be a nurse or a nursing assistant or on the housekeeping staff, like that guy with the tattoos who came through yesterday mopping the floor? I'm not sure.

I swing open the bathroom room and step inside, leaving the walker by the door. "See you later."

The nurse says, "Pull the cord to call for help if you need it."

Abby says, "Or call for me, and I'll help you."

I shut the door and sit down, alone for the first time in what feels like days.

Outside the bathroom, a man says in a gruff voice, "You again. What're you doing here?"

Abby says, "Leave me alone, you creep."

The nurse says in a harsh voice, "Go back to your room, sir. You have no business here. Only relatives are allowed to visit."

I flush the toilet and step out. "What's going on? I heard an argument."

I use the walker, and Abby takes my arm with a firm hand and helps guide me into bed. She says, "Nothing to worry about. It was just a confused patient who wandered down the hall."

I settle into bed and sigh. "He sounded angry though."

"He's probably in pain, like a lot of people here. Don't worry. He won't be back."

I study her features, where her beautiful mouth is pinched. She looks worried, so maybe she's keeping something from me. I wonder what it is. "Is something bothering you?"

She breaks into a wide smile. "Nothing, nope. All good. I'm the happiest I've ever been."

5

ELGIN

I limp down the hall, leaning on the walker, and stop outside Fishbone's hospital room, taking a look inside. The woman who hit me with a hammer in his apartment glares at me. She stands in front of the bathroom door, and a toilet flushes.

I scratch my armpit and scowl at her. "What're you doing here? You attacked me, and you should be in jail."

A nurse with yellow framed glasses and wearing blue scrubs says to me, "Please go back to your room. Only family are allowed to visit patients."

I say, "Why's she here? She's a cleaning lady."

The nurse smiles. "She's family, that's why. They're married."

As I turn to go, Fishbone comes out of the bathroom and pushes a walker. I saw him the day he borrowed money from my boss, and he looks half-dead compared to that healthy man. He gives me a blank look and smiles at his wife.

The nurse points down the hall. "Please go back to your room."

I say to Fishbone, "I'll be back. You owe a lot of money."

She shuts the door in my face, and I frown, shuffling down the hall with the walker. I'd better heal up fast from my injury, or my threats to Fishbone will be empty.

I slide into my bed and lean back on the clean pillow with a contented sigh. I located the deadbeat borrower, so that's a step in the right direction. A cart rolls down the hall, and the aroma of fresh-cooked food wafts into the room. It's dinner time, and I'm looking forward to a hot meal.

I pull out my phone and text my boss. 'Found Jack Fishbone. I'll get him to cough up the money soon.'

JACK

When I come out of the bathroom, Abby is talking to a big dark-haired man who is using a walker. He's wearing a hospital gown, robe, and yellow socks, so he must be a patient. He glares, but I can't think of a reason why he'd have a beef with me. I'm not his doctor or involved in his care. Maybe he was confused and ended up in my room.

I say to Abby, "Step one accomplished. I made it to the bathroom on my own."

She wraps her arms around me. "How about taking a short walk, a few steps down the hall? It'll help you get stronger, so you can come home with me."

My head aches, my knees tremble, and my legs are weak. I grip the walker and say, "Let me rest up first. I need a nap before taking a stroll."

"Whatever you say. You're the one who came back from the dead."

She helps me settle in bed, pulling up the covers to my chin. I say, "Thanks, sweetheart. I'm lucky you're here."

I nod off and dream of someone chasing me for money. I wake with a start and blink. My heart is racing, and my hands are slick with sweat. Abby is sitting in a chair working on her laptop.

I clear my throat. "Who was that guy I saw when I came out of the bathroom?"

She looks up. "Him? No one. Just a patient who was lost."

I furrow my brow. "He looks a lot like someone in my dream. That's odd."

She goes back to work, tapping on the keys. "Uh huh."

"What're you doing?"

She shrugs. "Just a hobby of mine."

I realize I know nothing about her, except she says we were close friends for many years. I hope I haven't made a mistake by diving in and marrying her. I say, "Which hobby is that?"

"Just fooling around with the stock market."

I swallow hard. She had said I was in debt. "I hope you can handle money better than I must have before I hit my head."

She chuckles. "I can assure you that I am definitely better at managing my investments than you were with money."

"Will we have enough to get by until I find a job? I

might not be up and around right away, like the doctor said."

She closes the laptop and comes over, taking my hand. She kisses me on the cheek and says, "Don't worry about that. Just get better so you can get discharged. We will definitely be just fine."

"What did I spend money on? Did I give too much away to charities? Is that why I was in debt?"

She bites her lip. "No, Jack, it wasn't that. You bought too many pairs of limited-edition high-end sneakers."

I start to sit up, but piercing pain in my head makes me stop. I groan and put a hand to my temple. "Man, that hurts. Can you ask the nurse for something for my pain?"

"I will."

As she walks to the door, I say, "Why sneakers, of all the things I could've bought? And why go into debt for them? It doesn't seem smart. Did I wear them?"

She shakes her head. "You wore flip flops and kept the shoes in your second bedroom. Come to think of it, I need to sell your shoes and use the money to pay off your debts." A concerned look flits past her face, but she presses her lips together.

I say, "What were you about to say? Let's not keep secrets between us."

"Fine, I didn't want you to worry, but one of the people you borrowed money from has a hired man who collects debts, and he's the man down the hall."

I shrug. "That's not a big deal. We'll talk to him and work it out."

"This is bigger than that," she says. "He's violent and angry. I hit him with a hammer when he choked me at your place. Your neighbor, Mr. Abernathy, shot him with an arrow from a cross bow, and that's why he's in the hospital. They had to remove the arrow from his leg during surgery."

My mouth falls open. "That's a lot to take in, especially when I don't know who Mr. Abernathy is. I shouldn't have put you in danger by not paying a debt. How can I pay it back?"

She sighs. "Irena was working on that for you, but someone stole the gold sneakers. We still have the rest of your sneakers to sell, so I'll work on that, now that we're married. But it isn't one debt we're talking about. You had many."

I cringe. What a flake I was. "That's embarrassing." A vague thought tickles at the back of my mind. "Do I have a computer? Maybe that'll show hidden money in bank accounts."

"Your computer was taken by the FBI for evidence in an upcoming fraud trial against Craig."

"Who is Craig?"

"Our friend from high school."

My jaw drops. "What about my stuff? Where did my things go? Maybe they're worth money."

"The jerk you just saw, the big, hairy man with the

walker, he choked me and wrecked your furniture. There's not much left but a broken sofa, a smashed bedframe and a slashed mattress. But Irena, Kelly, and I took your sneakers, so he didn't get those."

I squint, processing the information. "Was he looking for something?"

"The FBI thinks he was searching for money and passwords to offshore bank accounts. Craig was in your apartment too, looking through your things."

I let out a weary sigh. "This is a lot to take in, and I'm sorry that I roped you into this. You sound like a responsible person, and I appreciate you being patient with me when I'm lying here helpless." I chuckle. "You're being patient with me, the patient."

"Very funny, Mr. Fishbone. It's the least I can do for my friend who is now my husband."

An aide bustles in and sets down a tray with a small milk carton on it. Abby lifts a domed lid, revealing a dinner plate with salmon, rice and broccoli. Abby says, "Thank you," to the aide and turns to me. "Pretty fancy food for my favorite patient."

She pushes a button to make the head of the bed go up. I say, "You must be hungry. You can eat half."

"Go ahead and eat. I'll grab a bite to eat in the cafeteria and be right back."

I hold the fork and worry about the debt collector down the hall. "What'll we do about the money I owe that man? I don't want him to hurt you."

She picks up her purse, flashing me a smile. "We'll figure it out. I'll be right back. And if he shows up in your room again, push the red call button and ask for the nurse to help."

She places the remote by my left hand and goes out the door, leaving it open.

6

ABBY

I slip out of Jack's hospital room and stride down the hall, glancing covertly into each room to find the creep who choked me. I won't let him threaten Jack or ruin our new life together. I'll warn him off, and if I have to strike a bargain with him to keep Jack safe, I will.

In the last room on the left, he's in bed surfing television channels. I go in and close the door behind me. He turns, and his mouth falls open. His eyes grow wide.

I point at him. "Don't mess with Jack. We need three weeks to sell things to come up with the money he owes."

He shakes his head. "Our business would fail if we handed out favors to people like you. Besides, the longer you wait, the more interest adds up. Your new husband hasn't paid back a dime, so I'll be a permanent fixture in your lives until his cash comes in. And don't try to hide, because I'll find you, wherever you run. You'll end up paying far more than if you coughed it up today. Be smart and pay me now."

My hands clench. "We need a few more weeks, that's all."

"Not an option, doll, but nice try. Pay the money."

"It's not his fault he's late paying you back. He's hurt. He didn't even know who he was until I found him. He has amnesia from a traumatic brain injury."

He rolls his eyes and mutes the television game show. "Cry me a river. Everyone's got a sob story, but yours tops all. My boss says no excuses. If I have to break your husband's legs, I will. Face it, you married a loser who didn't pay his debts. My employer sends me the delinquent cases. She likes to prove a point by having me hurt people. It makes a statement, you know?"

My stomach knots, and my armpits prick with sweat. "Don't hurt Jack, whatever you do. I'll work out a plan to pay your boss back."

He grins. "We don't offer payment plans. Pay the full amount with interest or someone gets hurt. It's your choice. Maybe he'll have an accident in the hospital, a nice little slip and fall, and no one will suspect I was involved. Or, I'll make it happen at home. He'll trip on a throw rug or fall down stairs. Which will it be?"

I gulp. "We'll come up with the money. How much does he owe?"

He looks up at the ceiling, stroking his whiskered chin. "Adding interest and late payments to the original amount, plus processing fees, it comes to eighty thousand dollars, and it's going up daily."

I snort. "There's no way it was that much. He had mentioned fifty thousand dollars to me in the past." When Jack had wanted to buy a pair of Bill Bowerman hand-made running shoes with the original waffle sole sneaker, I told him I wouldn't chip in or lend him the money.

He says, "He borrowed much more than fifty thou and took advantage of our easy lending policy. Sixty thousand dollars plus fees and other stuff comes to eighty thousand if you pay today. The amount goes up tomorrow."

I clench my fists and stamp a foot. "That's outrageous. We don't have eighty thousand dollars to give you."

He points a finger at me. "You're not giving it, you're paying it back, two totally different concepts. And remember, he didn't have to come to us. He could've not borrowed money. It was your husband's choice to enter into this binding relationship."

I frown because he's right. Jack got himself into this predicament, and I hope he'll be a new man by the time he recovers from his head injury. I want him to forget his habit of hoarding limited-edition athletic shoes. Irena divorced him over his spending habits and how he didn't hold down jobs. But he'll be different with me. I've been in love with him since high school, and I'll stand by his side, helping him along the way, like right now.

I clear my throat. "I'll see what I can do. What's your name anyway?"

"Elgin Johnson, like the FBI case in the 1950's where an agent was murdered. What's yours?"

I turn to go. "Figure that out for yourself."

He clicks the remote and canned laughter fills the room. "That's not a problem."

I step out in the hall and lean against the wall, taking slow breaths to calm myself. I've got to come up with the money and protect Jack from harm. I'd like to ask him how much he really borrowed, but he lost his memory. The FBI has his computer, and I can't check there. Maybe Irena knows. They were close, and Jack may have told her.

7
____

IRENA

I knock on Jack's hospital door and say to Kelly, who is beside me breathing through her mouth, like she does when she's nervous, "I hope he's still here." She nods, and my pulse quickens as I step inside. The room smells like salmon.

Jack sits in bed with his head in his hands. A white bandage is on his head. His hair is short and uneven, which he might have done with kitchen shears in the marsh before boarding Buzz's boat and heading to the wharf. The area around his eyes is bruised purple and black. He's thin and looking older than forty years old. The patient in the hospital bed is a pale ghost of the party animal I knew.

I wince and wonder if he'll bounce back to being the man we loved. I'm sure Abby is doing her best helping him recover. It puzzles me that they were married, and I wonder if a marriage is legal when a person has memory loss. I'll ask Jack a few questions to see if he's of sound mind.

I push aside a partly eaten dinner on a tray and perch beside him on the bed, resting a hand on his bony shoulder. "Hey, Jack, how're you doing?"

Kelly stands, shifting from side to side, crossing her arms.

He says in a hoarse voice, "Who are you? I don't like you sitting so close, so please stand up and don't stare at me."

I step to the window. Kelly comes over, standing shoulder to shoulder with me. He has to remember his own daughter. "We're family," I say, turning to look at the blanket on the foot of the bed and not his face. "I was once married to you, and this is your daughter, Kelly, who you loved with all your heart."

He frowns. "I married Abby Love. I don't remember being married to you or having children, but I want to have them. If you were my family, you would've been here at the hospital when I was brought in, and you would've been by my side helping me. No one was here. I was all alone until Abby came."

Kelly coughs. She goes in the bathroom and closes the door, but I can hear her sobbing.

I say, "Jack, can't you just fake it until your memory returns to make her feel better? She's only thirteen. She needs her dad, so give her a hug and say you love her?"

He shakes his head. "I can't do that. It wouldn't be right. I want to be honest with everyone from now on. No more lies."

My chest tightens. "What did you lie about?"

He stares at the floor. "Money, I guess, because Abby says I'm in debt. A man down the hall says I owe him money, and he wants to hurt me."

I cringe, recalling the man who broke into Jack's place and choked Abby. "Is he big and hairy? And he has a gravelly voice?"

"That sounds like him. Abby went out for food, but it's been a while. I wanted to try walking, but I'm pretty weak. I need her help."

I go over to the end of the bed and open my arms. "I can help you. We can walk a few steps together."

He pulls the walker closer to the bed. "No, it has to be Abby. I don't know you. You say we were married, but it doesn't feel like it. I'll wait until she comes back."

Kelly comes out of the bathroom, wiping her eyes. "Dad, I can help you try to walk. My name is Kelly, and I love you, even if you don't remember me."

I hold my breath as she takes his hand in hers. She says, "I'll just hang out here for a bit, and we'll get to know each other. Is that okay with you?"

He studies her hand. "I guess that's okay. You seem like a sweet girl."

A few minutes later, Kelly says, "Try to stand and lean

on this walker. Mom and I will support you. Don't worry, we won't let you fall."

Jack stands and sways from side to side. He sits and says, "I feel dizzy."

Kelly sits by him and says, "You've been through a lot."

I say, "Do you remember anything that happened when you hit your head?"

He blows out a breath. "I don't. It's a blank, but everyone asks me that."

I say, "We're concerned."

"If you cared, why weren't you at the hospital with me before this?"

I open my hands. "Abby and Buzz and I didn't know where you were. The hospital had you down as a John Doe."

He winces when I mention Buzz. "If Buzz is my friend, where is he? I haven't seen anyone by that name. You could've called the hospital. I was all alone."

Kelly says, "That must have been scary. Buzz was your best friend, and he was Mom's boyfriend until a while ago." She shoots me a look, and I shrug.

He groans. "I'm wiped out. I'm need to sleep. Help me lie down."

We get him settled, and the door swings open. Abby comes in carrying a cup of coffee and a brown paper bag. The smell of a beef burrito fills the air. When she sees us, she freezes in place and looks from Kelly to me. "I didn't expect to see you here today. Next time, give me a heads up and text first, okay?"

She sets down the bag and coffee, rushing to Jack's side. She lowers the head of the bed, pulls up the covers, pats his arm, and he closes his eyes. She turns to us and says, "He looks worn out. What did you say to him?"

Kelly glances at me, and I say in a low voice, "I asked if he remembered anything about when he hit his head."

"Questions like that remind him he lost his memory and make him sad. He wants to remember but can't. So, don't bring it up. Just tell him about your day and take his mind off his horrible predicament and pain. They cut into his skull, you know, and removed a piece of it."

Kelly and I cringe.

Abby whispers, "There was too much pressure on his brain from the blunt force trauma he experienced, and it was life-threatening. They think someone hit his cheek and eye, and there's a severe injury to the back of his head. The poor man."

Kellys says in a quiet voice, "I'm glad you're with him. What can we do to help?"

Jack stirs in his sleep, moaning.

Abby glances at Jack, then at us and says, "We have a huge problem, and I need your help with it."

8

ABBY

My hands turn cold, and my heart races. I say to Kelly and Irena, "The man who tried to kill me at Jack's place is a patient in this hospital, and he's right down the hall."

Kelly's face pales. "The man who choked you is here?"

I flick my gaze at Jack to be sure he's sleeping and say in a low voice, "Yes, his name is Elgin Johnson, and he'll hurt Jack unless we pay what's owed."

Kelly shudders. Irena slips an arm over her shoulders and says, "How much money are we talking about?"

My stomach sours. Raising enough money on a moment's notice is an impossible task. If I sold my investments, it would take a minimum of three to five business days for the funds to be available, and that's optimistic. I say, "Eighty thousand if we pay today, more if we wait until tomorrow."

Irena's jaw clenches, and she crosses her arms. "That's a crazy amount of cash, but I'll do what I can."

Kelly whispers, "We can't let him hurt Dad."

The three of us hug. Our body warmth is a fire that fuels my anger at the debt collector down the hall. If I'm being completely honest with myself, I'm ticked off at Jack. How in the world did he dig himself into so much debt? That won't happen on my watch. He'll be different when I take him home. I say, "Let's come up with a plan."

Irena says, "This is a classic Jack move, letting others clean up after him."

Kelly nods, but I say, "Hey, no bad mouthing. That's my husband in bed. It's not his fault he's out of commission. Besides, I love him. I've always loved him."

Kelly smiles, but Irena's mouth falls open. She says, "You sure were covert about caring for him. I never suspected it."

I grin. "I hid it pretty well, and he did too, until this happened."

Kelly whispers, "Wait, you and my dad were a thing, but we didn't know?"

"That's right. But let's talk about the money problem and how to get Elgin Johnson off our backs. Let's brainstorm ideas. The first thought that comes to mind is one I won't write down. We don't want to leave a trail for authorities to follow or end up in trouble with the Feds."

Irena says, "You mean snuff Elgin Johnson out? End his life?"

Kelly and I motion with fingers over our mouths to quiet down. Kelly says, "Mom, keep your voice down."

Irena puts her hands on her hips and says in a low voice, "We can't eliminate the threat. They'd just send someone else, and Jack does owe the money. So, offing Elgin is off."

I say, "We need to find a way to get the money together. I think I can take a cash advance on my credit cards for forty thousand, but the interest will be painful to pay. And we still need to come up with the other half."

Kelly says, "We have to keep my dad alive."

I motion to the window, and we move over so as to not wake Jack. I glance outside, looking over town at the winding river. Down below, a train roars by on the tracks, heading north. If only those people knew how lucky they are not to be ailing in some way and not to have their lives threatened by money collectors. I gaze at Jack, who is sleeping with his mouth hanging open.

I say, "Irena, do you have any ideas for how to get forty grand today?"

She makes a sour face. "Why isn't he in prison for choking you? He shouldn't be out in public."

"Maybe they'll arrest him when he gets out of the hospital. Or maybe the cops are too busy, given the increase in crime."

Kelly says, "We should tell those two FBI agents who came around and talked to you, Mom. Maybe they'll do something."

I nod. "It's possible." I search my pockets but don't find the FBI agent's card.

Irena digs in her jeans pockets and holds up a card. "I'll call them when we finish talking."

She flashes a smile, and my shoulders settle, surrounded by support. Jack and I will get through this troubled time with the help of our friends. Except for Craig, that is.

An idea comes to me, and I hold up an index finger, saying, "This is an odd thought but maybe Craig's parents would help us. Jack is partly in trouble because Craig forced him into calling innocent, older people, and convincing them he could invest their money."

Irena taps a finger on her chin. "It's worth a try. I heard Craig's parents didn't bail him out of jail because they wanted to teach him a lesson. He's being held until the trial, and his funds are frozen."

I say, "Okay, here's a plan, and we'll divide up the tasks. Kelly, will you start a RunFundMe page to collect donations for your dad, to help him get back on his feet? Irena, why won't you sell the rest of his sneaker collection right away."

They nod. I point to myself. "I'll go ask Craig's parents to help us. It's their son's fault that Jack was hurt, because I bet it had something to do with the scam. Maybe Craig did it. Perhaps they'll feel sorry for Jack and chip in money. Or they could loan it to me with interest. It won't likely work, but I've got to try."

Someone knocks on the door, and a nurse with yellow-framed glasses and blue scrubs pushed in a tall rolling cart with a computer. She goes over to Jack and says, "I need to check your vitals."

Jack opens his eyes, and I say to Kelly and Irena, "Let's see how he is and then get out of here."

9

———

JACK

My eyes flick open, and a woman with yellow-framed glasses and blue scrubs stares at me. My armpits are damp with sweat. I say, "Where am I?"

She says, "You're in the hospital for a head injury. I'm going to take your vitals."

She clamps a device on my index finger and runs a hand-held monitor over my forehead. She turns to a computer on a tall cart, her ponytail swaying, and types on the keyboard.

Abby stands by my side and pats my hand.

The nurse says to Abby, "He might be disoriented at times, so be patient with him."

I grimace, because I want to be healthy and have a sharp mind. I don't want to burden my wife. I swallow, but it takes a few times to get it down.

The nurse says, "I'll take your blood pressure." She wraps a cuff around my left arm and watches as it inflates, tightening around my bicep. I'm too weak to defend myself if I got into a fight. Instead, I'm a blob with a sore backside from sitting on a thin mattress.

The nurse frowns. "Your blood pressure is elevated. I'm sorry, but I have to ask everyone but family to leave."

Abby and the other two look at each other and smile. A woman says, "I'm his ex-wife."

A teenage girl says, "I'm his daughter, but he doesn't know it."

She looks like a kid who has her act together. I search the corners of my mind but can't retrieve crumbs of memories about this girl. She isn't shy around grown-ups and gets along with Abby, which matters. I vowed to be a better person, if I didn't die on the operating table, and it was a fool's bet, because no one can bargain with death. Now, I smile at the kid and decide to be kind to her.

Abby says with a smile, "And I'm his wife. We're all family."

The nurse's gaze flits over the group, and she says, "Keep the noise down, so Mr. Fishbone can rest."

I clear my throat and say, "Call me Jack. Mr. Fishbone is too formal." My skull throbs, and I squirm. I say, "Can you give me something for the pain?"

She says, "I'll ask the doctor. How was your trip to the bathroom? Did you urinate?"

My face heats. Sitting in bed surrounded by people

and feeling vulnerable in a hospital gown, I probably stink like a dumpster during crabbing season. I wonder if I can stand in the shower and clean up on my own. Or will I have to accept help? When I get out of the hospital, I'll lift weights and get in shape. I'll jog. I'll floss every day and brush my teeth after each meal. We'll close the chapter where I was hurt and move on to happier times.

I clear my throat and say, "Yes, but no number two."

The nurse taps on her keyboard, entering information. "You haven't eaten in days, and your bowels may be sluggish. When you go home, I recommend you take a stool softener."

I cover my face with my hands. When I become a nurse technician or whatever they call it, I'll understand what patients are going through, after being on this side of the medical system, facing death.

The nurse says, "Are you finished with your dinner?"

Most of the food is left on the plate. I shrug and say in a hoarse voice, "Yeah. It felt like it got stuck in my throat."

She removes the tray, takes it out to the hall, and comes back for the cart. "Call if you need me. And try to walk, using the walker."

Abby says to the nurse, "There's a patient down the hall who was giving Jack trouble. Can you stop Elgin Johnson from coming in our room and harassing us? They know each other before, and Jack owes him money. Elgin wants it back right away."

The nurse puts a hand to her heart. "I'll bring it up in

our staff meeting during shift change. We don't allow patients to be threatened. This is a healing environment, and people need to be safe. It seems cruel to demand money from a man who lost his memory."

Kelly says, "We're starting a RunFundMe page on Meadow Book, so people can donate and help my dad, if you and the people who work here want to help him."

The nurse nods. "I'll donate, and I'll spread the word. I'm working a twelve-hour shift, so I'll be around for a while, and I'll be back tomorrow. I'll let the police know Elgin Johnson is causing Jack trouble. They came here to interview him, because he choked a cleaning lady in Millersville. I heard she defended herself with a machete and a bow and arrow."

Abby's eyes grow wide. "That was me, I was the cleaning lady. Elgin Johnson broke the door down and smashed things with a baseball bat when I was cleaning Jack's apartment. He was crazy angry."

The nurse says, "That must've been horrible."

Abby touches her bruised neck. "It was. He slit the couch cushions and mattress, and the rest is smashed. The place is a wreck."

I say, "My stuff doesn't matter. At least I'm alive."

Irena says, "I have the junk collectors coming tomorrow to clear out the stuff. The landlord needs the apartment, and rent was overdue. Craig was paying it, but he's in jail."

My pulse picks up, and a high-pitched alarm goes off,

beeping. Blinking lights on the blood pressure monitor flash with a warning that says my blood pressure is high. The nurse stabs buttons and resets the monitor.

She says to me, "I want you to take a deep breath and let it out real slow."

I inhale, let it slowly out, and repeat the process. I say, "Who is Craig? Why was he paying my rent?"

Abby says, "Craig was our friend, but now he's in jail."

I frown and furrow my eyebrows. "I don't remember him."

Irena says, "That's fine. We'd better get going. We have a lot to do."

The nurse says, "Nice to meet you."

She rolls her computer into the hall, leaving the door open.

10

IRENA

A tall, broad-chested hairy man leans on a walker in Jack's open doorway, staring inside and glaring at Jack. Abby gasps and says to me, "There's that guy again. Jack owes him money." She stands in front of Jack with her arms outstretched, protecting him. She points at the man and says, "Go away."

He says in a gravelly voice, "Did you get the money? The deadline is by midnight tonight."

Abby's hands clench.

I say to her, "I'll take care of that creep."

Abby whispers, "Thanks."

I pick up the remote on Jack's bed and push the red call button. I march over to shut the door in Elgin's face, but he thrusts his walker in the room.

He says, "If Jack hadn't borrowed money and defaulted

on payments, I wouldn't be after him. If you want to blame someone, blame it on him."

I put my hands on my hips and throw him a death stare. "He's not in his right mind, so you can't expect to be repaid under these conditions. He just had surgery and doesn't know he borrowed money."

Elgin shakes his head. "It's not my concern. He signed a contract saying he'd pay it back on time, with no exceptions." He turns to Jack, who is gripping the bed covers. "Isn't that right? You signed your rights away when we doled out money. Maybe your new wife can bail you out of the problem you created."

Jack coughs. He says to Abby in a weak voice, "I don't want to use your money. Just let him hurt me, and let's get it over with."

Abby shakes her head and says to Elgin, "He'll pay you back when he gets a job."

Elgin laughs. "When will that be? In fifty years?" He points to Jack and says, "He couldn't even work as a part-time bartender."

I march up to him, so close I smell garlic coming from his pores, and say, "Go back to your room. Let him rest."

A short nurse strides into the room. "Is this man bothering you?"

I nod. "He's upsetting Jack. Please keep him away from this room."

She guides Elgin down the hall. "If you bother that patient again, I'll report you."

He says, "I was just being friendly, visiting sick people." They move down the hall out of hearing range.

I turn to Jack. A tear rolls down his cheek, and he says, "I'm too weak to defend myself, and I can't protect you three. I'm a waste of humanity."

Abby says, "You'll get better. This is the hardest time. We'll get through it."

Kelly steps to his other side and takes his hand in hers. "Don't worry, Dad, we'll help you get better. Until you can protect yourself, we'll do it for you."

I say, "We're here for you. Just focus on getting better."

The nurse comes in and says, "I'm going to order a swallow test."

Jack coughs. "What's that?"

She says, "You may have dysphagia. Sometimes brain injuries can lead to difficulty swallowing. If you cough or choke when trying to eat, you could inhale food down the windpipe, which can lead to pneumonia. We have to take every precaution in serious cases like yours."

Jack's lips quiver. "I just want to get better, so I can be like everyone else."

I study him, because the old Jack I knew thrived on being different. His brand of uniqueness called for outrageous behaviors, like the time he took me on a hike in Washington Park on a Sunday afternoon in high school. He turned off on a faint path that led up a cliff. I stopped and pointed at pebbles on a steep slope, a seemingly impossible summit to climb. I said, "That's not safe. I'm not going up there. I'm going back to the car."

His eyes lit up at the challenge. He opened his arms wide and said, "That's the reason we should do it, because no one else will. Our whole lives are ahead of us, and we can do anything. We can climb this cliff. We can start a business. We can hike the Wonderland Trail's ninety-three miles around Mt. Rainier." He grinned, waving his arms for emphasis, but I pointed to the trail. "I'm going back to the car. See you at the lookout. Toss me the keys."

He closed his eyes and threw them with such force that they sailed over my head and down the steep edge behind us, down, down, down, into the blue water of Burrows Bay. I looked out and squinted, as if the keys would magically fly back into my hands. But all I saw was the lighthouse keeper's cabin on Burrows Island. To the west was Rosario Strait, where rumrunners ran bootleg whiskey at night during Prohibition. I pursed my lips because Jack and I were about to have a dry spell. It was my car and my car keys he'd carelessly tossed away.

I said, "You know what? Let's take a break from each other. We're too different to be together. I'll find a ride home and see you at school, but don't call or stop by."

He crossed his arms. "Fine, have it your way. See you at school."

I hiked out to the paved two-mile loop road, burning up anger in my haste. My heart thumped with each step as I mulled over how close friends can fall apart. When I reached the boat launch, I leaned against a tree and called Abby for a ride.

She pulled up in her white sedan with a dented bumper, and I hopped in, saying, "That's it. I'm done with Jack. Remind me of that if I ever decide to change my mind."

She met my eyes for a fleeting second, and I saw a glimmer of hope before she looked back at the two-lane road. I shook my head, telling myself I was imagining things, and turned up the radio. We rolled down the windows and belted out songs as if it was our last day on earth as seniors with a month left of school.

A few days later, Jack appeared on the front lawn of the high school during lunch when I was sitting with Abby by the flag pole. He bent on one knee and said, "Irena, will you forgive me for insisting on getting my way? Let's get back together and pretend this never happened."

My throat was dry, and I set my baloney sandwich on a brown paper bag on my lap. Licking mustard off my right index finger, I considered his plea. Our mutual friend Buzz and I got along really well, and he might be a better match for me than this impulsive hot-headed guy with an infectious laugh.

He put his hands together. "Please?"

Something in his gaze made me feel seen. He grinned, and laughter burbled up from inside me. I said, "Fine, let's try it and see how it goes. But I'm not following you up a cliff, no matter what."

He chuckled. "You never know where we'll go. We're about to chart our future."

I smiled, because I had hopes and dreams. I wanted to own a business, be my own boss, and fix things. If it involved boating and repairing engines, all the better.

We exchanged a quick kiss, and he left for drama class. As he turned to go, Abby watched him with a look of longing. I said to her, "Did you want to go out with Jack? Did I step on something you wanted to happen?"

She bit her lip and shook her head, looking down. "No, it's fine. It's all good."

But there was an awkward moment as we gathered our things and headed back into the building. Now in the hospital, I give her a smile. She's holding Jack's hand and finally has what she wanted all those years ago.

"Okay," I say to Abby, Kelly, and Jack. "We've got to run home, so I can sell the rest of the sneakers. Kelly will set up a RunFundMe page on Meadow Book for donations. We've got to work fast because we need the money by midnight."

Jack says, "People shouldn't give their hard-earned money to help someone like me. I didn't save and was a selfish person. I'll bear the brunt of the consequences."

Abby pats his arm. "Hon, Elgin will hurt you if we don't come up with the cash. I can't let you get hurt or killed. I just found you."

Jack leans back and closes his eyes. "Fine. And thanks."

Kelly says, "Bye, Dad."

He opens an eye. "Bye, Kelly. Thanks for helping me."

She smiles. "Of course. That's what family is for. We help each other."

Kelly and I stride down the hall, and I pat her shoulder. "I'm so proud of you."

She looks at me. "I'm proud of you. I thought you'd be jealous of Abby and Dad being together, but you seem fine about it."

We step into the elevator. As the elevator descends, I say, "I'm getting used to it. Your dad deserves happiness, and so does Abby. Who am I to be negative about it? They're good together."

BUZZ

I pick up my pace and walk the dog with a million ideas racing through my head. Jack is in the hospital, and I need to return his wallet without anyone finding out what happened. Jack's place has been picked over, with Irena and Kelly going through his things. But maybe I could stick the wallet in a pile of clothes, and it would disappear out the door when the junk guys get there. No one will find it.

I say to my dog, "Kelly loves you, old boy, and Irena will ask us to move back in soon. I'm sure of it." But even as we round the corner to my home, I have doubts. Who am I to predict the future? I need to come up with a plan to win back Irena's heart. Let's see, step one: Create trust. Step two: Make her laugh. Step three: Give a gift to Kelly, so Irena's heart melts. The trouble is, I have no idea what to buy.

I unlock the front door and step inside, toweling rain off my dog before he shakes and water, spraying the nautical chart mounted in the entryway. For Irena, I could write a few poems, bind them in a leather notebook, and offer them as a special sign of my earnest intentions. For Kelly, I'll pick out a book at the store that she'll love. A wide smile spreads across my face. This is the solution for winning back love, through parchment and paper and well-chosen words.

I step around books stacked on the floor and kick off my shoes. A wave of yearning washes over me, and I dig in my pocket for a metal key. I walk to the second bedroom closet and unlock the door.

Turning on the light, I say to the framed photo of Irena taken when she was young, "Hello love. Before long, we'll be back together. I know in your deepest heart that you're waiting for me."

I strike a match and light a candle, kneeling at the alter to the one I love.

"Irena, you're mine, and I'll always be yours. I love you, sweetheart."

Pulling out a pen and paper, I jot down a poem and place it alongside others in a white leather notebook. I'll show them to her when I have the courage to let her peruse the lines dredged from deep in my soul.

11

IRENA

We head home, and I heat frozen salmon burgers in a frying pan, tossing in chopped Bok choy. I wash the cutting board and tilt my head, puzzling over how Abby doled out assignments for us to drum up money, when in the past, I was the one in charge. She is Jack's advocate, but before this, he leaned on me for help. Who would have thought a rogue wave sweeping over Jack and me would change everything within our group of friends.

I set dinner on the kitchen table, and Kelly pushes her device aside. We eat in silence, with palpable tension in the air. We don't have much time to save her dad from harm. I swallow a bite and say, "I'm not used to Abby telling me what to do."

Kelly gets up and puts her plate in the dishwasher. "You're in the back seat, not driving the bus for once."

I stand. "Let's get going. We don't have much time."

She sets my plate in the sink. "I wish Dad hadn't borrowed so much money."

I blow out a breath. "Me too, but we have to help him."

"I don't think it's realistic to expect to come up with the money by midnight tonight. There's no way."

I make a face. "You're probably right, but we've got to try."

Two hours later, we're sitting on the couch tapping away on laptops. I started auctions for three pairs of Jack's sneakers. Kelly launched a RunFundMe page on Meadow Book and asked for donations on social media to help her dad. She stretches her arms, and I say, "We can do this. We Fishbone gals get things done."

She giggles, and I chuckle. We glance at each other and erupt into peals of laughter. I wipe my eyes and sigh. Thank goodness for the sanity-saving existence of my daughter during this mess.

Kelly blows out a breath. "I wonder how Abby is doing, asking Craig's parents for money to help Dad."

I say, "She might get a door slammed in her face."

ABBY

I pace in Jack's hospital room and rehearse what I'll say to Craig's parents when I see them. To support to him, I'd better get going to knock on Craig's parents' door and make a plea for money. I wrinkle my nose. How crass, to go begging for cash.

If I call them first, they might refuse to see me, so I'll be better off just showing up. Buzz knows Craig's mother from a book club at the bookstore, so I text him. 'Is Craig's mom in town? I want to stop by but won't bother if they left for Arizona.'

I roll my eyes because when winter hits, many residents over age sixty flee for warmer temperatures. They run in November from rain, gale force winds and gray winter skies, returning in April on an annual migration. By Thanksgiving, if you're stuck in Millersville, wind and rain lashing your face, you're a turkey who forgot to leave town.

Buzz texts a minute later. 'She's home. Happy to hear about your marriage.' He adds a smiling emoji. If I had time to hire a full orchestra to celebrate my marriage to Jack, I would. When I'm not worrying about the man down the hall hurting Jack, I'm breaking into smiles and bursting with our nuptial news.

I pat Jack's arm. He opens his eyes and says, "You're here. It wasn't a dream."

I whisper, "We're in a very good dream that's real. I'm so happy about that."

He starts to cough and puts a hand to his throat. I take the remote, push the call button, and wait. "Don't worry. We'll get help."

He nods but doesn't answer, making a zipper motion across his lips like when we were teenagers revealing secrets at Fir Island. We used to go there at night during high school after sneaking out of our houses. I would climb out of my second-floor window and step on the porch roof, inching to the edge and swinging my legs down. My stomach churned, but I didn't look down as I climbed down the trellis and dropped to the lawn below. My father would have been angry about my antics if he saw me, but he fell off a ladder and died when I was young. As a result of seeing him fly past my bedroom window, flailing his hands and yelling in fear, I'm afraid of heights. My father's final gift was a fear of going above the ground floor.

In high school, my friends and I took Craig's Boston Whaler to the island in the evenings, where we'd dare each other with wild feats. A full moon was shining over the water one night. The sea was calm, and a hush fell over the water. We docked by the old run-down restaurant and climbed out of the boat. Buzz and Irena tied the dock lines while Jack and I carried a cooler filled with beer.

Craig led the way and stopped at a dirt path at the far end of the building that was closed for the night. The dark forest loomed ahead. Jack and I set down the cooler.

Craig said, "I dare you to climb a tree higher than the second floor of the building. Bet you can't do it before me. Race you there."

He took off running into the forest, but I stood still, my stomach burning with acid. Irena raced off after Craig, with Buzz following in her wake. Flashlights emitted yellow bands of light, bouncing with each step, in the thick grove of fir and cedar trees.

My hands turned cold and clammy. I wanted to run like the others, but I stood like a statue, frozen in fear.

Irena yelled, "I win."

Buzz said, "Winner, winner, chicken dinner."

A warm hand slid into mine, fingers interlacing. Jack said in a soothing low voice, "I got you, Abs. I know you're afraid of heights. Let them run around while we go find a place to talk. Okay with you?"

I said, "Okay."

We found a protected spot under a cedar tree's boughs and sat facing the water. My body trembled, and Jack patted the ground in front of him. He said, "Lean against me, and I'll lean against the tree. You're shaking. Tell me what's upsetting you so much."

That night, while the others ran in the dark forest, issuing dares and challenges, I watched the bright almost full moon rise over the trees beyond the bridge and told Jack about how I saw my father die. He said, "That's awful. Now I get why you don't want to go off the high dive at the pool."

I whispered, "Don't tell anyone, okay?"

He said in a low voice, "Your secret is safe with me. This is just between us."

Irena called, "Abby, where are you? Are you okay?"

Jack whispered in my ear, and a shiver ran up my spine. Hairs on my arms stood on end, and goosebumps pricked the flesh on my legs. He said, "I'll slip away. Pretend you don't know where I am."

I stood, leaving Jack's reassuring warmth behind, and said, "I'm here. I'm fine."

In a flash, he was gone without making a sound, stepping with stealth. Irena came up and wrapped me in her arms. "Hey you, I was worried when I didn't see you. Have you seen Jack?"

I shook my head. I saw her clearly in the bright moonlight, and I averted my eyes, looking down. "Nope, haven't seen him."

She cocked her head. "You were out here all by yourself?"

I shrugged. "Sure, just needed time alone is all."

Irena turned and cupped her hands. "She's over here. She's fine."

Buzz ran over, and Craig followed. Buzz said, "I was getting worried."

"Me too," Craig said.

Jack jumped out from behind a tree, threw up his hands and yelled, "Surprise!"

We screamed, with my voice carrying the loudest because the act of recalling my dad dying had put me on edge. We laughed, and I shook out my legs. Buzz and Craig slapped Jack's back. "Good one." "You got us."

I said with a smile to Jack, "We never can trust you, Man of Stealth."

We stood there talking about what to do next, and a twig snapped nearby. I looked around, but we were all accounted for. A sense of dread washed over me.

Buzz said, "What was that?"

Craig shrugged. "Must've been a deer."

Irena said, "But they bed down at night."

I whispered, "Let's get out of here."

Craig said, "Meet you at the boat. Every man for himself."

We ran to the boat, climbed in and forgot about the cooler with beers we'd brought. When we were beyond the bridge and heading into the marina, I blew out a breath. Jack sat in the stern next to me, his thigh warm against mine. Irena sat on his other side, snuggling up to him. They'd been going out for a few months by then.

I listened to little waves slap against the sides of the boat as the engine thrummed, bringing us back from the danger that lurked on the island, real or imagined, caused by us or who knew what else. I crossed my arms and vowed, as I eyed the bridge, to ignore my attraction to Jack. I had to move on because Irena was my best friend, and I'd never do anything to hurt her or tread on her new relationship.

Now, a nurse comes in Jack's room, and I say, "He sounds like he's choking."

He nods.

The nurse checks his vitals and elevates the head of his bed. She says, "Keep the head of the bed up, so it'll be easier for him to swallow."

She leaves, and I check on Jack's breathing. He seems fine, or at least enough so I can leave, so I kiss his whiskered cheek. "I'm going to go round up money to keep the debt collector away from you."

Jack says in a hoarse voice, "Don't go. I'm worried you won't come back."

"I'll be back, Mr. Stealth. Just get some rest."

He closes his eyes, and I pull on a coat, pick up my

purse and laptop bag, and stride down the hall. It'll take me forty minutes to drive to Millersville, at least ten to talk with Craig's parents and another forty coming back, depending on traffic. Begging Craig's parents for money may be a fool's errand, but I must save my husband.

12

JACK

The nurse wakes me and says, "Let's get you up and walking around, so you can be discharged when the time comes. By the way, the doctor put in an order for a swallow test." I sit on the edge of the bed but break into a coughing fit, shoulders shuddering. It takes me a while to swallow my saliva.

She brings the walker over and pats the metal handle. "Where's your wife?"

"She left to run an errand." I stand and shuffle forward, gripping the walker and taking tentative steps.

The nurse says, "Are you okay?"

I grit my teeth and push the walker ahead. My feet throb, and my knees tremble. I release a shaky breath and say, "As fine as can be expected." I don't want to tell the nurse that I owe a lot of money to a man down the hall. She wouldn't understand my predicament. "Did you tell the staff to keep that man Elgin out of my room?"

She nods. "Yes, I did. Patients should feel safe in the hospital. Any disagreements you two may have should be handled outside this building."

A tickle at the back of my throat makes me clear my throat. I say, "What if I wake up one day and don't like who I am or where I live? I don't know what I'll do then."

I shuffle ahead, and she says, "That may happen, but it's best to take it day by day. Why worry ahead of time?"

We step into the hall, and I lean against the wall, breathing hard.

She says, "Let's get you back to bed."

Hairs on the back of my neck rise, and I have a feeling someone is watching me. I glance at a large hairy man down the hall. He is leaning on his walker and staring at me under dark bushy eyebrows. A shiver runs up my spine. I shuffle into my room and climb into bed.

A trickle of sweat runs down my arms, and I ask, "Any chance I can get a shower?"

"Yes, I'll get someone to help you."

I'm panting from walking a few steps. I hope Abby will be successful raising money, while I lie in bed, utterly useless.

A short man wearing blue scrubs and orange sneakers comes in and opens a door. Something about his orange shoes tickles at the back of my mind, reminding me of a piece of my past, but I can't call it up.

He says, "I'll help you bathe. Let's go to the shower room."

With his help, I use the walker, hobble into a tiny tiled room, and pull off the hospital gown. He tosses it in a plastic bin.

I shiver, wishing I didn't need help to take a shower. He turns on the water and puts his hand in, testing the temperature. He says, "Okay, you can get in. I'll help you, but take it slow and don't get your head wet."

I step into the shower and moan with pleasure as warm water pounds on my chest. My back muscles relax. I scrub my armpits with soap and smile as water beats down. Standing in the shower, I let my hands fall to my sides and appreciate the feeling of being clean. It's a small step on my road to recovery and re-joining the human race.

The nurse technician reaches over, turns off the water, and hands me a towel. When I'm dry, he gives me a hospital gown. I smile, feeling better. I'll get stronger, leave the hospital and have a future with my wife.

He guides me back to bed and says, "A patient down the hall asked me to give you a message. Mr. Johnson said he's looking forward to seeing you when you're out of the hospital. He said you guys play poker, and it's time to up the stakes."

My stomach knots. I gaze into the man's brown eyes and see no malice. He doesn't know he's delivering a message from a dangerous thug. My heart races, and I break into a coughing fit, gasping for air and clutching my chest.

The nurse technician leaves the room to get help. I wipe my mouth with the back of my hand and calm myself by thinking of Abby. She mentioned my best friend is Buzz, but I haven't seen him here. If he is such a close friend, why hasn't he shown up?

13

ABBY

I pull up to a large brick waterfront home in Millersville near the Cedar Island ferry dock. Our close friend Craig grew up here, and during high school we spent many afternoons and weekends hanging out in a room above the garage. I'd look out the window at the ferry and wonder if I'd ever live in a place as nice as this when I grew up. I live in a studio apartment, but one day I'll upgrade my address.

I close my car door and walk up a paved path. My hands are cold, and my pulse picks up. Craig's mother was kind to me, but I'm not sure that will still be the case, given Jack was an FBI informant providing evidence in Craig's upcoming fraud trial. When I ring the doorbell of the mansion, chimes sound inside.

A woman's voice comes through an intercom. "Can I help you?"

"Yes, I'm Abby Love. I'm here to see Craig's mother."

A minute later, the front door is thrown open, and Craig's mom appears, throwing her arms open wide. "Abby darling, how wonderful to see you, but in such awful circumstances. Come in."

I follow her to the kitchen, and she gestures to the live-edged wooden table by the window with a water view. "Take a seat. I'll get us something to drink. Beer? Wine? Something stronger?"

"No thanks, I've got to keep my head on straight with all that's going on."

She tilts her head, and her blond highlights reflect light. Her black yoga pants and top are snug on her fit frame. A gray cardigan over her thin shoulders completes her look. I've always envied the way her commanding presence radiates power with undertones of kindness and concern.

She says, "Coffee? Tea? Or water?"

I massage my temples. I'm embarrassed to ask her for money when her son is in jail, partly because of Jack's information about the scam. I take a breath and tell myself to be strong for my husband's sake. "Coffee, please. And thanks for seeing me. I'm sorry to just drop in like this."

She waves a hand and turns to the coffee maker. "Nonsense, I always told you kids this was your home too and to stop by whenever you could."

Minutes later, she slides a cup of steaming black coffee

in front of me. "Milk or cream or sugar?" She laughs. "I doubt I have any of that in the house though. I just got back home from a trip."

"Black is fine," I say. "Thanks. Where did you go?"

She pours a glass of water from a filtered jug in the refrigerator and sits beside me. She sighs. "You'd think we'd never want to leave this fabulous view of the water, but after what happened to Craig, we wanted to escape from town for a while and take our minds off our troubles. We went to Palm Springs, but I ended up coming home early. We're not getting along so well."

I say, "What's going on, if I may ask?"

She runs her fingers through her perfect hair. "I wanted to post bail so Craig can come home and live with us until his trial. But his father refused and said he needed to learn a lesson and stop getting into trouble with the law."

I nod, because in the past Craig's parents hired attorneys, so charges didn't stick.

She taps a manicured fingernail on the table and says, "Our son doesn't belong in jail. It was just a little white-collar crime."

My eyebrows shoot up, and I swallow a sip of coffee. It burns on the way down my throat. "But he set up a system to rip off old people, pretending it was an investment."

She waves it off. "He was getting interest on the money before paying it back with a premium. He just didn't have time to make the payouts before he was arrested. He means well. I hope he doesn't mix with the wrong crowd in jail. It could make his problem worse."

I say, "His problem?"

"He's always had a drive to be rich and to prove himself at any cost. He wants to be wealthier than us. But we weren't an overnight success story. Craig's been trying to amass huge amounts of money in schemes. This isn't the first time something like this has happened."

I hold the hot mug in my hands and gaze out at Cedar Channel, where a ship with a blue hull is being guided by two tugboats. Across the way is Cedar Island.

She dabs tears from her eyes with a tissue. "What would you do if you were in my position? Would you bail him out or leave him to learn a lesson?"

I set down the coffee cup and cross my arms. "It's complicated."

She nods. "It sure is."

I bite my lower lip and consider her question before answering honestly. "If I were his mother, I'd bail him out. He's been in there long enough. It seems harsh to leave him there if you can post bail."

She stands. "That's it, that's what I'll do. Your visit was perfectly timed. I'll go ahead with my own money and get him out." She takes her cell from the counter and puts on reading glasses, stabbing at buttons, dialing someone. Before she hits the last number, she looks at me, and her eyes grow wide. "I'm sorry. I don't mean to appear rude, but I want to get going with this. What is it you wanted to talk about?"

I get up from the table. "One of Craig's friends is having a tough time financially, and we're trying to raise money to help him."

Her forehead creases, but I charge ahead. "I know this is a big request, but would you be willing to donate all or part of what we need, which is forty thousand dollars, by midnight? We're starting a RunFundMe page for the fundraiser."

She puckers her mouth. "I'm sorry, but it's out of the question, in light of my decision to post bail for my son. My resources are spoken for. Family first, you know." She flashes a forced half-smile.

My stomach clenches. I botched the request, and it's my fault, but I had to be honest with her. "I understand, and if I were you, I'd help my son first. It's just that our friend will be hurt if we don't come up with the money by midnight tonight."

She says, "You always struck me as a courageous young woman who would do anything to defend her friends. I'm sure you'll come up with a way to raise the money. Who needs the money? Is it Irena or Buzz?"

I swallow, and my ears click in the uncomfortable silence. My idea to come beg was a bad one, and I'm out of ideas for who to turn to for help. I clear my throat and say, "We're raising money to help Jack."

Her mouth falls open. "But I thought he was missing."

"He was, but I found him in the hospital. He has a traumatic brain injury, and he lost his memory, but believe it or not, we were married in the hospital."

She pats my shoulder. "I'm happy for you. I never completely trusted Irena, because I thought she played with Buzz and Jack's affections, laughing at Jack's jokes but staying close to Buzz."

I say, "Irena and Buzz finally got together, but she broke up with him over Jack going missing. Buzz helped Jack disappear, and that made Irena angry."

She taps a finger to her lips. "Sounds like there's a lot of drama going on with your friends, but that was always the case during high school. My husband and I blamed Jack for roping our son into a scam, but I've been mulling it over and think it's possible Craig was the one running it, like the FBI says. Anyway, please let yourself out. I have calls to make. It was good to see you."

I move my cup to the sink. "Thanks for the coffee. I hope next time I see you it'll be under different circumstances."

She waves goodbye to me and says on the phone, "Hello? Yes, dear, I've decided to post bail for Craig. It's the right thing to do, even if you don't agree with it. Your tough love policy had time to work, and now I'm going to bring him home."

I tiptoe to the front door and a small trophy on the fireplace mantle in the den catches my eyes. The gold shines, reflecting light. My fingertips tingle, and I imagine tucking it under my coat and walking away with a token of a wasted trip. Old urges return, dancing in front of my eyes. Take it, a voice whispers in my head. Take the little trophy and hide it at home. It'll make you happy.

I tap a toe and deliberate, counting the seconds, like my counsellor recommended. Drumming my fingers against my thighs, I force myself to turn to the threshold. I'll leave without succumbing to temptation. I'll turn over a new leaf in light of my fresh start with Jack.

I step outside, inhale salt air coming off Cedar Channel and stride to my car. With the cash advances I took on my credit cards, I have half the amount needed to pay Jack's debt. A year ago, Jack wouldn't have let us sell his prized collection of sneakers. But now it's time to save his life and keep his bones intact by parting with his precious items.

I climb in the car and call Irena. She answers and says, "I can't talk now. Too much going on." She hangs up. I drive away and hope she's working her magic, because otherwise, we're screwed.

14

ELGIN

I stare at my phone, letting out a low whistle. Fishbone's daughter is all over socials trying to raise money for her dear dad. I gave ten dollars to her RunFundMe campaign, just to show what a nice guy I am, and watched the money roll in, more with each passing minute.

The daughter tells a whale of a sad story, and she's bringing in the bucks, so I figure I should raise the bar and keep extra for myself. Skim off the fat, as they say. My boss will never know I held some back.

My phone dings with an incoming text. My boss texts: 'Status update?'

I reply: 'Applying pressure. The deadbeat's sick, but his relatives will pay it off.'

She writes, 'Keep me posted.'

I put my phone down and turn up the television volume to catch the local news.

A blond reporter in her thirties is wearing a blue raincoat with the hood pulled up, standing in front of a fast-flowing river. She says into the mic, "We have a live update on the missing man from Millersville. Stay tuned for breaking news."

I click off the TV and get out of bed, hobbling to the window that faces west. Down below a muddy river winds around a bend. My deadline for Fishbone's payment will be like a rising river, where people make adjustments or get damaged in the process. I grin because my motto should be: You pay to play, or you pay with your life.

I scratch my belly. I need to tell Fishbone and his family about my changing the payment deadline, but the nurses won't let me in his room. I'll leave a comment on the daughter's fundraising post. Then I'll linger outside his room and catch his new wife going inside. Seeing the fear in her eyes when I break the news will give me a jolt of adrenaline and bring joy to my heart.

A nurse knocks and comes in. "Good news, you're being discharged."

My mouth drops open. "I didn't expect it so soon."

She says, "It'll take a few hours to process the paperwork before you can leave."

I screw up my face. I want to stay and monitor Fishbone from down the hall to keep the pressure on. There are many things I'd like to do to him, but I need him alive to collect the cash. I say, "My leg still really hurts. Can't I stay just for tonight?"

She shakes her head. "Doctors' orders. We need the bed for another patient."

I get up and use the walker, dragging my leg. My acting is good, but the pain throbbing in my thigh is real. "I've got to see a buddy down the hall before I go."

She blocks the doorway and crosses her arms. "We can't let you go in Mr. Fishbone's room."

I hold up a hand, keeping one on the walker. I'm an expert in telling a sob story. "He'll want to see me. I swear it on my sister's grave."

The nurse cringes. "We can't allow it."

I open my hand and say, "Would you please give his wife a message from me? She'll want to reach me tonight."

She tilts her head. "I suppose I could do that, as long as you're not talking to the patient or harassing him."

"Do you have a piece of paper?"

She pulls a pad out of her pocket and a pen.

I jot down my cell number, adding, 'Time moved up to eleven, not midnight.'

Handing back the pad, paper and note, I say, "She was going to give me a book about gardening and how to grow the best beets. Thanks. I appreciate it."

The nurse leaves, and I hobble down the hall.

I grimace as a jolt of pain shoots up my leg and pause

to catch my breath, leaning on the walker. When Fish-bone pays up, I'll take a well-deserved vacation. Costa Rica and Portugal both sound good. Or I could get off the grid and hole up in a cabin in the woods.

15

____

BUZZ

I step away from the bookstore front counter and browse the aisles, searching for a book to give Kelly. Passing the joke books that Jack liked to read, I remind myself to visit him at the hospital. I want to see how he's doing, and if I don't show up, it might look suspicious. Stopping in the poetry section, I chew on my lip. What if he sees me and remembers how he hit his head?

I swallow hard. I could be charged with attempted manslaughter. The night he disappeared, I should have just dropped him at the wharf, stayed on my boat and turned around, taking off for town. Instead, we said goodbye on a dirt road by the derelict cannery, and when he said he wanted to take Kelly and Irena with him, I lashed out. I was fed up with everything being all about him all the time.

I pause in the poetry section and take a slim book of

Walt Whitman poems off the shelf. I hum to myself as I gift wrap it. Taking a card with Orca whales, I jot down a note: 'For Kelly during a difficult time. Poetry soothes the soul. You are loved by everyone you know. Buzz.'

I take my dog, who came with me to work, and we hop in the car, heading for the hospital in Mt. Vernon. A half-hour later, I park at the hospital, and we trot to the front door. Jack likes dogs, and my pup's presence will make the visit less awkward and provide a distraction. If someone barks about my dog coming in, I'll take Happy to the car and leave the windows cracked open on a cool evening. He's a people-pleaser, with his wide smile. And his being there will give me an excuse to leave early.

We step in the elevator and get off on the eighth floor. My hands tremble. I have been drinking too much coffee and dreading this moment. I slip into Jack's room, where he's in bed, looking pale and worn. Abby isn't here, which is a relief. I want to spend time with Jack without Abby monitoring our conversation or seeing a flash of guilt in my eyes that might make her realize my near fatal mistake.

I cringe and look at him, lying with closed bruised eyes in a hospital bed with a white bandage around his head. What I did to my best friend in a flash of fury was unforgivable.

I move to the far side of the bed, away from the door, so it will be less obvious my dog is in the room. When I point to the floor, my dog sits, his tail swishing back and forth. Happy nuzzles Jack's hand, and Jack opens his eyes, saying in a hoarse voice, "When I get out of here, I want a dog. Is this one mine?"

I say, "This is my dog, and his name is Happy. You've always liked him."

"Can Abby and I have him? We'll take good care of him."

I shove my hands in my pockets, because there is no way I'll give up my dog, even if it is my fault that Jack is hurt and in the hospital. "I'm sorry, pal, but I can't be parted from him. I'll help you pick out a dog though, when you get out."

Jack looks up from the dog. "I don't know your name. Who are you?"

I wince. "Hey, man, it's me, your best friend Buzz."

He pets the dog and coughs. "Sorry, I don't remember you. I seem to have lost my memory."

Jack rubs my dog's head. "Nice dog. I almost remember a dog like this." A look of worry flashes across his face.

I hold my breath and hope he'll remember our good times and not the fight at the waterfront. My face heats. I lashed out, but now I'm filled with regrets. Only an animal would leave their best friend for dead. If Irena knew what I did, she'd never speak to me again.

Jack's purple black eye is swollen. He has a hard time swallowing. Now that I see the damage I inflicted, I must find a way to make up for my grave mistake. I clear my throat. "I'm sorry you're laid up like this. It must be awful."

He groans, running his fingers over my dog's ears. "It hurts, you can't believe how much." He coughs, hacking away.

"Do you want the head of your bed down? Anything I can do to help?"

"No. The bed's fine, but my body isn't. I just want Abby to come back."

I rest a hand on my acidic stomach and blurt out a question that is seared into my mind. "Do you have any idea how you were hurt?"

He stops petting the dog and fixes his gaze on the ceiling. "Everything is murky. But I have a feeling someone close to me betrayed me. Who do you think that was?"

His brown eyes bore into mine, and for a second, I wonder if he's putting on an act and he knows what happened, down to the moment my fist struck his face. I turn to the window to take a break from feeling impending doom descending. My chest is tight. I want to unload my secret about what happened, but there is no one I can talk to without getting turned into the police. I say, "I have no idea."

Jack falls asleep, and with his eyes closed, he looks sixty years old instead of forty. I'm about to leave when a nurse in blue scrubs comes in and says to me, "I'm going off shift, and I'm supposed to give this to Mr. Fishbone's wife. Can you give it to her?"

I hold out my hand. "Sure, I'll give it to her." I shove it in my pocket.

She peers over the bed. "Dogs aren't allowed in the hospital, so you'll have to leave. Also, only family can visit. Mr. Fishbone is recovering from a difficult surgery."

I nod. "Understood. See you later, buddy."

He moans and says, "If you see Abby, tell her to come back."

"Will do, my friend, take care. I'll be sending you positive thoughts."

Two aides in blue scrubs enter the room. The nurse nods to them and says to Jack, "They're taking you to have a swallow test."

Jack coughs and tries to catch his breath.

I say, "Hang in there. I'll see you later."

Jack blinks but doesn't look at me. I click my tongue to signal it's time to go to my dog, and Happy and I take the elevator to the ground floor. Abby is coming through the parking lot and heading my way.

My face heats with shame at how I caused Jack's brain injury. I'm the lowest of the low. I hurry around the corner and hide behind a rubber plant, bending over petting Happy.

Abby peers around the corner. "Buzz, is that you?"

I stand and nod.

She says, "I thought I spotted Happy. Did you see Jack?"

I blow out a shaky breath and shove a hand in my

jacket pocket, where Jack's wallet reminds me of my misdeeds and malignant behavior. "I brought Happy to cheer him up, but we got kicked out. It's only family for now, I guess."

She eyes me, and I scratch my chin, hoping she won't guess what I did at the wharf. I gulp and reach into my pocket, holding out Jack's wallet. My demented pleasure in keeping his wallet evaporated the moment I saw him in bed. My fever dream of embracing my bad side is over, and I'm back to being a boring bookstore owner who would never unleash his temper.

I say, "I found Jack's wallet by the cannery. Here, you take it and give it to Jack."

Her eyebrows furrow, and she takes the wallet, opening it. "Looks like everything is here. I'll cut up these credit cards though. He doesn't need to get in more debt than he already is. Why did you go to the cannery?"

I shrug. Happy leans against my leg, and Abby kneels down, petting him. I take a moment to gather my thoughts and hope she won't spot holes in my story. I say, "I dropped him at Martin Wharf before he went missing. I went back to see if I could find clues about where he'd gone."

She says, "That makes sense. Hey, we're raising money to pay off one of Jack's debts. He borrowed from question-able people and their enforcer will hurt Jack if we don't pay back the money by midnight. Will you chip in and donate?"

My throat goes dry, but I manage to say, "How much do you need?"

She glances at her phone. "We need an additional forty thousand dollars to pay it off, and we have four hours until the deadline."

I clear my throat. "I'll give five hundred, if that'll help."

She pats my shoulder. "Thanks, I appreciate that. Venmo me the money, okay?"

"Will do."

She walks away, and I lean against the cool wall, letting out a weary breath. The mess Jack was in before he went missing is even messier, and it's mostly my fault. Guilt rests on my shoulders, and I trudge outside. My dog thinks I'm a fine human, but I know otherwise.

16

———

KELLY

I post on socials about the fundraiser for my dad, and money starts to pour in from my pleas. An hour later, we've raised almost eight hundred dollars. I say to my mom, "People are giving, but we have a long ways to go."

She comes over and looks at my screen. "They gave that much already?"

"Yeah." I read a comment about the fundraiser. "But someone says Dad didn't pay his debts, and what happened was his fault. They put an angry face emoji."

Mom puts her hands on her hips. "That's rude, but in a way, they're right. Your dad was in debt, and there's no reason anyone should help him. Did you mention he lost his memory?"

I shake my head. "I thought that was private and would bring out the crazies."

She shrugs. "Add it and mention your dad's in the intensive care unit. Put that in the post."

"Sure, I can do that." I edit my post, but a minute later, the person, who goes by Elgin, posts another comment: 'This guy is a grifter from way back. He should've had healthcare insurance to cover his expenses.'

I cringe, and Mom squints at the screen. I click to hide the comment. We can't make the truth vanish, but at least it gives Dad a fighting chance. I overheard Abby say to Mom that if we don't get the money by midnight, Dad could get hurt or worse. I've got to save him.

Typing on the keyboard, I edit my original post and add details about how sick he is and how he's getting kicked out of his apartment. People don't need to know he didn't pay rent or hold down a steady job. To save my father's life, I'll tell a partial truth. I mention how he is re-learning to walk, and he's having trouble swallowing. My computer dings with incoming messages. Donations are up to a thousand dollars, but it isn't nearly enough.

I say, "Mom, isn't there anyone else we can ask for money?"

She sighs. "I wish there was, but I can't think of anyone."

I smile. "What about Grandma Jacklyn?"

She shakes her head. "She just got out of Shore Lodge. It wouldn't be right to bother her. Besides, her son took most of her money. I keep my distance from him, the way he glowers. He gives off a bad vibe."

"We should call her anyway. She'd want to know what's going on."

Mom nods. "Okay, but let's make it quick. We have a lot to do."

I pick up my phone. "I'll text her before we call."

She chuckles. "People over age sixty expect the phone to ring without someone texting first. I've been meaning to call her anyway to see how she's doing."

We call Jacklyn Stone, who is my honorary aunt. Mom met her at the garden store, and they became friends. It rings, and I squirm in my seat. I'd feel better if she came over. She feels like warm cocoa in a mug on a cold day. She's reassuring and comforting, with a steel hard core.

I smile when I hear Jacklyn say, "Hello?"

"Hi, this is Irena and Kelly. We've been thinking about you and wanted to catch up, but we've had a lot going on. How are you?"

"Just peachy," she says. "Never been better. I'm fit and ready to rumble and doing my fifty pushups a day. I've even added planks. Got to stay fit. But enough about me. What about Jack? Did you find him?"

I say, "Abby found him in a hospital in Mt. Vernon. They had him down as a John Doe because he didn't know who he was."

Mom says, "He has a traumatic brain injury. He can't remember anyone except Abby, and they were married."

"Well, congratulations to him for picking a wonderful woman as his wife. I bet they'll last many years, like my marriage to Albert. But how are you two holding up? It can't be easy. This sounds like a fruit basket upset."

I smile at Jacklyn's odd phrase. But then I say, "Dad doesn't know who I am. He forgot he has a daughter."

"Come over, and I'll give you a hug. You can spend the night in my extra bed and I'll smother you with affection."

Mom says, "We can't stop over because we're working on a deadline to pay back money Jack owes or he'll get hurt. The amount will go up if we don't get it by midnight tonight."

Jacklyn says, "Who is doing this to you? Let me at them, and I'll straighten them out. Anyone with a heart would give Jack and his family a break. For heaven's sake, he doesn't even know his own name."

Mom says, "It's no use protesting because Jack signed an agreement and borrowed money from the wrong people. And then he didn't pay it back in time."

Jacklyn says, "I'm sorry to say this, but he was a fool. Cover your ears, Kelly, I don't want to offend you. Did he borrow money to pay you the back child support due?"

I say, "He bought shoes. And he bought Mom a violin before he left."

Jacklyn says, "So you're busy raising money before midnight?"

Mom says, "That's right. Abby took out cash advances on credit cards, so that gives us twenty thousand. I'm selling his sneaker collection, and Kelly set up a fundraiser. Do you have any ideas for what else we should do?"

"Sell the violin. And didn't he have part ownership with Buzz in a boat he didn't use? Get the money for that, if you can."

Mom says, "I'd hate to sell the violin. I only just got it. But you're right about the boat. I'll ask Buzz if he can pay us Jack's part."

"Good luck, you two. Call if you need more help. I'll lead a protest down Main Street, if that'll help. I'll sign off now, I'm in the middle of an online yoga class."

Mom hangs up, and we look at each other. Mom says, "Selling the violin is the right thing to do under the circumstances. I don't like it, but I'll do it. Maybe my teacher, Mercury Thunder, will know what it's worth. I'll text him and ask him."

I say, "Do you want me to ask Buzz about paying us for Dad's part of the boat?"

She smiles. "Thanks, sweetie, that would be a big help."

I pull out my phone and text Buzz. We're in a tight spot, and time is ticking down. Dad needs our help.

17

IRENA

I text the violin teacher asking the value of the violin and where to sell it. When I check the time on my phone, my pulse picks up. An auction I set up for a pair of Jack's shoes closes in ten minutes. Drumming my fingers on the kitchen table, I watch as bids come in, each topping the last. I run my moist palms over my jeans and say to Kelly, who is sitting beside me at the kitchen table, "I can't believe how much people are willing to spend to get these signed sneakers."

"What was the last bid?"

I point to my laptop. "Four thousand one hundred dollars."

She leans over, studying the screen. "I wish Dad could see this. He was right, you know, most of his shoes are valuable."

I cock my head. "I wasn't saying they aren't. It's just that he bought them when we didn't have enough money for food, or a newer car, or a vacation."

She says, "When's the last time you took a vacation? You never talk about that."

I cross my arms and eye the bids coming in. "I might go to Portugal someday."

She half-smiles. "You wouldn't want to leave your boat and business for a week. Besides, everyone who has money in town is going to Portugal. You should go somewhere remote and undiscovered, and take me with you, like to a beach in Bali."

I roll my eyes. "Nowhere is undiscovered anymore. It's not like the old days."

She grins. "You sound like an oldster. Way back before we had electricity, we had to read by candlelight."

I smile at her and glance at the screen. "Thirty seconds left."

We lean in, watching bids appear in the final seconds. When the auction ends, she gasps and I jump up, my chair falling on the floor. "Six thousand nine hundred and twenty dollars!"

We put our hands in the air and dance around, laughing.

Kelly says, "Will Dad get hurt if we don't raise the money?"

I press my lips together. "That's what Abby said.

Unfortunately, this is just one of his debts. We have to come up with the money in three and a half hours."

She says, "I wish he was better with money."

"Me too, sweetie. Otherwise, we wouldn't be running around drumming up cash. Let me add this to my spreadsheet and check on the other auctions I'm running." I type information into a spreadsheet and say, "Okay, I'm finished with that for now. Let's see how your fundraiser is going."

I look over her shoulder at a RunFundMe page on Meadow Book. A photo shows Jack grinning, standing at the marina by the water, and wearing a blue Hawaiian shirt, shorts, flip flops and sunglasses.

I say, "He looks happy in that photo."

Kelly scrolls through the comments and frowns. "Someone else commented on the post and said Dad got what he deserved. I'll hide it so others won't see it." She clicks, and turns to me. "Why are people being so mean? We're just trying to help Dad."

I hold up my hands. "I don't know. Everyone loves your dad. It'd be like making fun of someone when their boat went aground."

She rolls her eyes. "Enough of your boating metaphors."

I point to the screen. "Other people are saying kind things about your dad. We've raised two thousand dollars so far. Good job, hon."

I stare at my screen, checking the other auctions I'm running to sell Jack's shoes. We're a long ways from raising forty thousand dollars by midnight to protect him from his past misdeeds. I wince and bite my cheek, because I'm not sure we'll make it.

18

ABBY

I clutch a cup of coffee and hurry to Jack's hospital room but stop in my tracks. His bed is missing. Biting my lip, I find a nurse at a work station in the hall. "I'm Jack Fishbone's wife. Where is he? Is he okay?"

She stops typing and gives me a look of concern. "They took him for tests."

"Can I join him? He's been through so much. He might want me there."

Her eyebrows arch. "Visitors aren't allowed in that area. You can wait in his room, or go to the cafeteria until he comes back. It should take an hour or so."

I say in a shaky voice, "Thanks." A flood of worry sweeps over me, reminding me of when he went missing. I go in his room and stand by the window, looking out at the winding river, and call Irena to check in. While it rings, I take a sip of tepid coffee and touch my sore neck, where the thug choked me. If Irena doesn't give me good news about raising the final forty thousand dollars we need, then I will march down the hall and have it out with the debt collector.

Irena picks up and says in a breathless voice, "What's going on? Did Craig's parents donate anything?"

I shake my head. "His mom is posting bail and getting him out of jail. They need the money to help Craig. So, no go on that front."

Irena says, "I hope Craig won't come by to yell at Jack in the hospital. That wouldn't be good for him."

I nod. "I'll do my best to stop him from visiting, but seeing Craig might jog Jack's memory. For all we know, Craig might've hurt Jack and caused his head injury."

Irena says, "Craig was ticked at Jack for turning on him. What happened the night Jack went missing? Buzz said Jack was fine when he dropped him at the wharf. Maybe Craig hit him."

"I'd like to know the truth. I'm watching Jack for signs that he remembers people. If Craig does stop by, it'll be a test to see if Jack reacts in any way. I can imagine Craig hauling off and belting Jack. He has a short fuse, don't you think?"

"He definitely does. Craig's temper is barely below the surface, like a rock that could rip a hole in your boat."

I groan. "Stop with the boating metaphors."

"That's what Kelly's been saying."

I smile. "Let me talk to her, and then I want to hear

how much you've raised. I took out two cash advances, but the interest will be steep. I hate borrowing money, but we've got to bail him out."

"We're doing everything we can, because we love him. Here's Kelly."

"Thanks."

Kelly comes on the phone, and her voice trembles. "Someone named Elgin is commenting on the fundraiser page for Dad, saying mean things."

I frown and stare at the river. "Like what? Read me what he wrote. Put me on speaker."

Kelly says, "Okay, let's see. Here's a comment from him that just came in. He says the deadline for payment has been moved up, and now it's eleven o'clock tonight. He also says the amount is now ninety-thousand-dollars."

My pulse races, and I clench my fist. "We had until midnight. He can't just jack up the amount due. There's no way we can raise that much money by eleven."

Irena says in the background, "It's impossible. We can't let this creep control our every move. Go down the hall and talk to him, will you? Make him understand we need more time and get the deadline moved to tomorrow."

Kelly says, "I don't think this Elgin sounds like the type to be flexible. He choked Abby, and he has a temper. We've got to do what he says, so Dad won't get hurt."

I squint at the floor where the bed should be and say, "I'll talk to him, but I doubt it'll do any good. Wish me luck. How much have you raised so far?"

Irena says, "Not enough. Go down the hall and tell him he'll be hearing from me if he doesn't let us have until noon tomorrow."

I shake my head. "He isn't a guy to bargain with. He uses brute force to get what he wants. He's an enforcer. And, let's remember, Jack did this to himself. He didn't pay back the money he borrowed from shady people, so we have to deal with the hand we're dealt. But I'll talk to him and try my best."

Irena says, "Do you want me to drive over and confront him?"

I shudder. "Definitely not. That might make it worse. He might move the deadline even earlier."

Kelly says, "Call us back and let us know what happens."

"I will. He's right down the hall, so it won't take long."

Kelly says, "How is my dad doing?"

I sigh. "He's not here. They took him in for some tests. He's having trouble swallowing, but it's probably no big deal. Don't worry."

I pocket my phone and step out of the room. As I approach Elgin's room, Jack is being wheeled down the hall in a bed, and I rush over to him.

A breathing tube is coming out of his throat. His eyelids flutter, and he squeezes my hand. Aides push the bed down the hall, and I follow, swallowing hard. This isn't the honeymoon I dreamed about. This is a nightmare.

JACK

My mouth is dry, and something is stuck in my throat. I peer down at a tube and tell myself not to cry in front of the aides.

Two people wearing scrubs push the bed in a room and set the brakes. Abby smiles and slips her hand into mine. She found me and told me my name. Without her, I don't know what I'd do.

She says, "We'll get through this. I'll help you get back on your feet."

I try to speak but nothing comes out, so I move my lips in a kiss.

She says, "I love you too, Mr. Funny Fishbone. You'll get better."

A dark mood descends over me, and I frown, worrying she'll leave me for someone who isn't sick. My sense of humor fled when they stuck a tube in my throat.

A nurse comes in with a helmet in her hands. She holds it out and says, "We need you to wear this to protect your head until the piece of your skull is put back in."

She hands it to me, and I take it, throwing it across the room. The helmet smacks into the wall with a satisfying sound. No way I'll wear that.

19

BUZZ

I check my messages and groan. Kelly texted asking for money because her dad owns half my boat, and they need the money tonight. "Fat chance of that happening," I say aloud. "I'm not Mr. Money Bags."

I text Kelly back, 'I'll see what I can do, but it's short notice. Give me a few months to come up with part of the cash.'

Kelly replies, 'The collector creep increased the amount and moved up the deadline. Now we have to raise ninety-thousand-dollars by eleven to help my dad.'

I reply, 'I'll see what I can do.'

Guilt kicks in, and I let the dog into the backyard in light drizzle. Mist rises from the grass. I pace in my kitchen, glancing outside at the darkening sky, trying to come up with a way to help Jack pay off this debt. I owe him this much and more. I just repaid my home equity line of credit, which I took out to buy Irena an engagement ring she didn't want. She said she wasn't ready. What an idiot I was to think a diamond ring would get her to say yes to marrying me.

Happy scratches at the back door to come inside, and I grab a towel, holding onto his collar while I dry him off. I toss aside the towel, letting him run in the house, and as he rubs his back on the living room carpet, an idea occurs to me. One thing I can do, if Abby agrees, is to give him my dog because he asked about it at the hospital. I know it won't help with his money situation, but it might help with his recovery. I can never repay the debt I owe Jack for losing my temper, but I'll make it my life purpose to make amends.

I get down on the floor and play with my dog, throwing a plastic bone toy. Happy retrieves it and dumps it on the floor, and I repeat the motions of throwing it. Given how busy I've been, he deserves heaps of attention. I ruffle his ears and say, "What do you think, old boy? If Abby agrees, do you want to go live with them?"

Happy sits and barks, which I take as his agreement. "You've always liked Jack. I'd miss you though. But I could come visit and take you for walks."

I feed him his dinner, which he scarfs down, and lean back against the kitchen counter. Glancing around my home, I shake my head. Nothing is new or fancy here.

I tap my chin. "Should I tap my line of credit to help

Jack? I hate to do it, but this is for a good cause. I'll never make it up to him, but it's a step in the right direction."

The dog laps up water and scampers through the house. I clap my hands as the dog runs from room to room and chases his tail. "You've got the zoomies. Good boy, keep going. You need the exercise, and Abby's apartment is small. We'll keep this idea between us for now because Jack's in the hospital, and they have a lot going on. I'll spring it on them when he gets better." I cringe. "If he gets better, that is." I knock on a wooden coffee table. "I really hope he will, especially for dear Abby's sake."

I call Irena, and when she picks up, I say, "The new deadline is crazy. There's no way we can raise that much money by then."

She says, "I know. Abby's going to go talk to the debt collector. It's not fair. We need until tomorrow at noon or next week. The deadline of midnight tonight was tough enough. Kelly's really upset, and she's worried about her dad."

My throat closes tight with tears. "Of course she is, the poor kid."

She says, "We're selling his shoes and running a crowd funding page on Meadow Book, but can you think of other ideas to come up with that much? I'd like to get this jerk out of our lives forever and never see him again."

My jaw tenses. "We'll find a way."

She says, "I'm going to sell the violin too, but I can't work magic and do it tonight. I want to find out what it's worth first, but I haven't heard back from the violin teacher."

I squint at a smudge on my kitchen window glass. "The violin teacher? What's his name? Jack mentioned him once or twice."

"Mercury Thunder."

I chuckle, which is a relief after all the tension rippling through our friends' group. "That's right, and I couldn't believe his name when Jack told me."

She says with a smile in her voice, "He wears a bow tie in his long beard. I think you'd like him. He and Jack had some shared secrets, but I have no idea what they are."

My shoulders relax at her warm tone of voice. I've missed hearing that, because ever since Jack went missing, she's been on autopilot dashing around trying to fix the messed-up situation. But while she's wrestling with one challenge, another one pops up, in our whack-a-mole new reality. I can't wait until our lives settle down, and we go back to the way we were, if that is even remotely possible.

"Hey," I say in a soft voice. "I've missed you."

"I've missed you too."

"What'd you say after all this is over, and Jack is out of the hospital, we go out for a nice dinner, just the two of us? Or I'll cook for you at my place. You can bring Kelly, if you want."

"Sure, sounds like a plan."

I grin. "I'll look forward to it. By the way, I can use my

home equity line of credit to help bail Jack out. The money is available."

"Are you sure you want to do that? It's his fault we're in the pickle we're in."

I chuckle. "Irena Pickle Fishbone is in a pickle."

She laughs. "It's pretty crazy, isn't it? I don't want you jeopardizing your financial health to save Jack. We can't have the two guys I've loved drowning at the same time."

I suppress a groan. "Thanks, babe. If I decide to go ahead in the next hour, I'll text Abby and tell her."

"She's talking to the guy collecting the money and trying to get the deadline moved to tomorrow. Maybe wait to contact her for a bit."

"Got it. Love you," I say, "give Kelly my love too."

"Bye."

We hang up, and I peer out outside. Wind is whipping trees into a frenzy in the backyard, making branches sway. This is not a night to go out, but I'd better get over to the hospital to help. I grab my home equity line of credit checkbook, old school style, and tuck it into my jacket pocket where Jack's wallet had been. What a relief it was to hand my bad luck talisman over to Abby. If I hadn't gotten involved in Jack's scheme to disappear, I'd still be with Irena. Jack's plan busted up my relationship, but I can only blame myself for losing Irena.

Glancing at the time, I pat the dog on the head, toss him a treat, and say what all dog owners say when they leave home. "See you later. I'll be right back."

ABBY

While Jack sleeps, I hurry down the hall to Elgin's room. I look inside, and my jaw drops. His mattress is stripped bare. They must have discharged him. How can I pay the money back if he isn't here?

I wipe away tears and plaster a calm look on my face before I walk into Jack's room, where he is sleeping. A machine hooked up to his breathing tube whines in the background, making it one more noise maker in the stark, small room. I inhale a deep breath and slowly let it out. This is not a time to break down. I must be strong for Jack.

I take my purse and head to the elevator to get a sandwich in the cafeteria. I'm drained and dredging from the bottom of my well of energy. I never imagined saving Jack would take so much effort.

FRANKIE

Frankie McNalley turned to her partner, Special Agent Mark Brick with the FBI, and said, "The fraudster in the scam case is being released from jail. His mother posted bail."

Brick said, "I thought his parents weren't going to help him?"

She shrugged. "Guess they changed their minds. If I were a mother, I would've bailed my son out, depending on what he did. But if it was murder, I'd let him rot in jail."

Brick grinned. "That wouldn't happen, because any child of yours would toe the line."

She said, "It'd be black and white at my house. I'd set rules, and we'd follow them. My way or the highway."

He cocked his head. "I don't think that's how it works with kids, but I'm no expert."

She shrugged. "What do I know. I'm single and don't even have a cat."

He said, "No cat lady jokes about you, then?"

"Someday I'll get a dog, and I'll buy a house that needs fixing up."

"Frankie for the downtrodden?"

She grinned. "That's me, fighting for justice and fixing what's wrong in the world."

He laughed. "You and me both. We're reading from the same book."

She tapped a finger to her lips. "About this case. Do we have enough evidence from what Fishbone gave us before losing his memory to make an airtight case?"

He said, "We have his written statement and recordings of interviews when he was our informant."

"Let's dig into his computer and make sure we didn't miss other evidence."

20

IRENA

I bite a fingernail and wonder what Buzz will do. If he taps his home equity line of credit to bail Jack out, Kelly and I will be grateful, but I wish Buzz didn't have to go in debt.

I frown. If I sell the violin, that might take care of the problem. My phone dings with a text from the violin teacher.

He texts, 'Don't sell your violin. You've always wanted to play. Call if you want to talk about it.'

My hands tremble, and I call the violin teacher. When he answers, I say, "Would you please buy the violin? We need to come up with the money to help Jack."

He sighs. "I'd hoped it wouldn't come to this. I told Jack to stay and face his problems. Running away wasn't right."

I nod. "He left a financial mess, and I've been clearing out his apartment."

He says in a low voice, "There might be another way to raise money. You'd have to come over here to discuss it."

I glance at Kelly, who is on her laptop replying to comments about the fundraiser for her dad. We're up to five thousand six hundred dollars, which is not enough. One of the auctions I'm running is approaching the deadline for bids, and another is thirty minutes away from closing.

I blow out a weary breath. "My daughter is with me, and we're busy raising money for Jack. Can you come over here?"

"Give me five minutes, and I'll be out the door. What's your address?"

I give him our address and hang up. Turning to Kelly, I say, "The violin teacher is coming over." Rain patters against the kitchen windows. Frowning at the dark night, I say, "Weren't you supposed to be working on a science project?"

She says, "I got an extension because of what's going on with Dad."

I inhale and slowly let it out. "I hope Mercury Thunder can help us, because otherwise we're screwed."

I heat hot water in a tea kettle and pour it into two mugs, handing her one. "Here's the deal. When you see the violin teacher, don't laugh or giggle. He has a very long beard."

She shrugs. "I'm interested in meeting anyone who knew Dad."

Someone knocks, and I go over to look out the window at the violin teacher. I open the door, and he steps in, pushing back the hood of a blue rain jacket. Rain drips on the floor. I say, "I'll take your coat."

He hands it to me, rain drops glistening in his long gray beard, and I hang his coat on a hook. Kelly comes in, and I gesture to her. "This is my daughter, Kelly."

He nods to her. "It's a pleasure to meet you. Jack talked about you. He thought you might want to play the violin I made, even though he left it for your mother. But he said you were passionate about dance classes. How it that going?"

Kelly says, "I haven't had much time for dance class since he disappeared. Can you help us? We only have until eleven tonight to come up with the money."

He says, "Let's talk about it."

I point to the kitchen. "We'll go in the kitchen. Kelly is working on fund raising on socials. And I'm selling his sneakers in online auctions, but we're way short of the amount we need."

He slides into a seat at the table, and I say, "Would you like a cup of tea?" He nods. "Is peppermint okay?"

His long beard looks damp and is minus the bowtie tonight. He says, "That'd be great. How much money do you need to raise?"

I pour hot water in a mug, add a tea bag and set it

before him. Glancing at Kelly, I say, "We needed fifty thousand more after Abby took cash advances on her credit cards."

He tugs on his beard. "Jack's debt begets more debt and burdens friends. It doesn't seem right."

I sit down. "Kelly's crowdfunding has raised around six thousand and selling his shoes brought in about sixteen grand so far. How much money do we need Kelly, if you do the math?"

She thinks for moment. "Twenty-eight thousand."

I rub my temples. "Which is a lot left to raise in a short time. Abby's going to talk to the scum bag who is threatening Jack to try and negotiate with him." My stomach knots. There's no way we'll get there by eleven tonight.

Mercury sips tea and sits back, drumming his long fingers on the table. "Twenty-eight thousand dollars is a lot of money to come up with in a short amount of time. What if you don't hand over the money? What happens then?"

Kelly's face pales. "The man collecting the money says he'll hurt my dad. I don't want that to happen." She wipes tears from her eyes.

Mercury says, "The thug increased the amount and shortened the deadline?"

I swallow hard. "Yes."

He leans forward. "I know and care about Jack, so I'm going to throw out a few suggestions. You can ignore my ideas if you want."

Kelly puts her elbows on the table. I shift in my seat, and the chair creaks as I say, "Go ahead, we're listening."

He counts on his fingers. "Option one, do nothing. Keep the money you've raised and use it to pay off Jack's other debts. But you'd have to get him out of the hospital and hide him for that to work."

I make a face. "He just had surgery. They removed a piece of his skull to relive the pressure, and Abby just texted to say they put in a breathing tube. I don't see how we can take him out of the hospital."

Kelly cringes and sits back, biting her lip. I rest a hand on her arm and say, "I'm sure he'll get better soon. He's getting the best care, and Abby is with him. She won't let anything happen to him. She told me she is guarding him with her life."

Mercury tugs on his moustache. "Aren't people with traumatic brain injuries usually sent to Harborview in Seattle? Why didn't they fly him there or send him by ambulance?"

I say, "EMTs made the call, and Abby says the doctors are optimistic about his case."

Kelly grips the table edge. "We don't know if his memory will come back, and that's what I care about. I miss him."

Mercury says, "He's a wonderful man with a great sense of humor and even though it may not look like it, he has a clear sense of right and wrong. He confided to me about going undercover for the FBI and risking his life to stop a scam on older people."

Kelly swallows and nods.

I say, "He told you more than he shared with us."

He says, "I suppose that's true. He said he needed someone to talk to in all honesty who wouldn't judge him, so I became his confidante."

I drum my fingers on the table and wish Jack had trusted me that much.

Mercury says, "Option one is out then. We won't take him out of the hospital and hide him from the debt collector. What does this thug look like, anyway? Maybe I've seen him around."

I say, "He's big and tall with broad shoulders, brown hair and brown eyes."

Mercury tilts his head. "That describes many men in the area. Tell me more."

"I bet he's walking with a limp because Jack's neighbor shot him with an arrow. He choked Abby when she was cleaning Jack's place."

Mercury winces. "So, he's a man who is used to getting his way."

"I think so." My phone dings with a message, and I check it. "Abby went to confront him, but he was discharged, and she doesn't have a way to contact him."

Mercury tugs on his beard. "So, this vengeful person is on the loose and could be anywhere. I'd like to have a few words with him to straighten him out, but it'll take time to find him. What's his name?"

My stomach churns. "His name is Elgin Johnson. The last time I saw him, he was talking to Craig on the side of a road."

He picks up his phone and sends a text before setting the phone down. "We may be able to track down his car and find out where he is. Then I'll have a talk with him."

I shake my head. "He likes to hurt people, so I don't think that's a good idea."

Mercury smiles. "I don't mind conflict. Believe it or not, I'm more than a violin maker and music teacher, but I don't advertise my past skills. Don't tell anyone I'm involved in this. Can you two keep quiet?"

Kelly and I say, "Yes."

He opens his hands. "Besides, I might not be successful, and we'll be back at the same spot, looking for twenty-eight thousand dollars by eleven, which is in what, less than three hours?"

A shiver runs up my spine. "Yes, and if you bought the violin, is it worth enough?"

He stands and waves a hand. "It'd be near the right amount. I have a reputation as a violin maker, and if you look inside, you'll see my signature. But there are a few problems with that. Problem one is I made it at Jack's request, and it meant so much to him. When his memory returns, he'll realize you sold it and feel hurt. Problem two is I gave the violin to him as a favor, so I'm not going to buy it back. If I did, it would take too long to get the money anyway. Besides, I want to stand up to this man and take him down a peg."

He pulls on his coat. "We're not backing down to this thug. We've got to stand up to him. If this doesn't work, I have another idea I'd rather not discuss. Thanks for the tea, and I'll see you later."

As I open the front door to say goodbye, a blast of cold air rushes inside. Closing the door, I rub my arms and say to Kelly, "Let's get back to work. I hope Mercury can accomplish miracles."

Kelly says, "I hope so."

We sit at the kitchen table, and I say, "I'd like to dump Elgin Johnson in the Salish Sea with a weight around his neck."

Kelly looks over and frowns.

I peer out into the dark night, wondering who I've become. Living out Jack's nightmare has made me hard and harsh, bringing out my worst traits. I scratch my ear, wondering what Mercury Thunder was referring to when he mentioned an idea he'd rather not discuss. This is the time to bring out all possible solutions and not keep secrets until too late. That's what got Jack into trouble in the first place.

21

JACK

I wake and blink at a tube coming from my neck that is connected to a whirring machine. My head throbs, my throat aches, and I'm confused. I grab the remote and press the red call button.

A middle-aged nurse with short brown hair comes in. "Can I help you?"

I try to speak but can't get the words out. I point at the tube and my mouth.

Her brown eyes fill with concern. "It takes practice to learn to talk. I'll see if I can find a speaking valve for you."

I open my hands and lift my eyebrows. I want her to tell me what they did to me.

She says, "You had a tracheotomy. They cut into your windpipe to provide an alternate airway for breathing."

I point at the tube and pretend to pull it out.

She says, "The doctor will come in later to check on you. Don't tug on it."

I slump back in bed. My butt is sore from sitting so long. I turn on my side, and a device near my chest pops apart, setting off a beeping alarm. I try to reconnect it with fumbling fingers, and the nurse comes in. She says, "I'll do it. Leave the cords alone from now on and don't turn on your side."

I gesture to the empty chair, wanting to ask about my wife.

The nurse says, "I believe your wife left for a bit."

A tear trickles down my cheeks. I want Abby here. I don't like having a tube stuck in my throat. I feel like I'm an alien.

Abby comes in and rushes to my side, taking my hand. I wonder what's happening with the money situation and make a dollar sign in the air with my index finger. She says, "Relax. We'll take care of it. Focus on getting better."

The nurse takes my vitals, and Abby says to the nurse, "Can he take a walk?"

The nurse says, "Yes, but I'll have to unhook some things first." She disconnects the breathing tube from a machine and places a device over the hole in my neck.

Abby sets the walker by the bed, and she says with a smile, "What do you say, let's take a spin around the block?"

I inch to the edge of the bed, and with her help, stand up. Shuffling ahead with weary steps, I lean on the walker.

My knees tremble, and I stop to rest. I wonder if Elgin the debt collector is in the hospital. I don't want to run into him in the hallway.

Abby frowns. "The creep down the hall was discharged, so you won't see him again, here or ever, if I have my way."

In the hall, I lean against the wall, my chest heaving from the effort. Tubes come out of my mouth and dangle from my neck. My skull pulses with pain.

Abby squeezes my arm and says, "When we get home to my place, we'll start looking at houses to rent or buy."

Her words wash over me, and I'm not sure what she's talking about. I'm a little dizzy from exertion and the idea of so much change coming ahead.

A doctor in a white lab coat with a stethoscope around her neck approaches us. "Mr. Fishbone? I'd like to take a look at you. Let's go in your room. I'm happy to see you're walking."

I shuffle into the room and climb into bed with Abby's help. A nurse connects the breathing tube, and a machine whirs.

Doctor Wang says, "We're concerned about the swelling on your brain, and we'll be keeping you in the hospital for observation a few more days."

She says some other things, and I close my eyes while Abby asks questions. Tears leak from my eyes. I want to be instantly well and go home with Abby.

Doctor Wang says, "I'll check on you tomorrow."

Abby says, "Can he eat with that thing in his neck?"

"No, he has a feeding tube."

The doctor leaves, and someone knocks on the door. A man says, "Hey, Jack."

I open my eyes, and a man flashes a forced smile. He was here earlier and said his name was Buzz. His eyes fall on the breathing tube, and he cringes. I glance at Abby, because I don't have the energy for visiting. But it's strange that I have no recollection of the man she says was my best friend. I guess I'll just have to wait for my memory to return. But whoever put me in the hospital has rendered me helpless. I cross my fingers and hope I'll recognize the person if and when I see them.

22

BUZZ

I drive to the hospital and drum my fingers on the steering wheel. Guilt thrums in my mind, playing an endless album of regrets. If I borrow to pay off Jack's debt to Elgin Johnson, that won't solve his financial problems because he borrowed from others.

I turn into the hospital parking lot and ponder the obvious question. Because I nearly took Jack's life on the waterfront that night, am I morally obligated to clear his debts, even if I must borrow money to pay them back? I shake my head and get out of the car, slamming the door shut. No amount of money will make up for my almost killing Jack. There is no negotiating, and my mistakes are stuck in the record book of my life.

I stride into the hospital and take the elevator. Knocking on Jack's door, I force a smile and say, "Hi guys, is this a good time?"

Jack stares at the ceiling with a forlorn look on his face and closes his eyes. A tube in his neck is connected to a machine. I shove a hand in my pocket and glance out the window. What have I done?

Abby says, "Come in. The doctor just said Jack needs to stay in the hospital longer. They're concerned about the swelling on his brain."

I nod and walk to the window, leaning back against the window sill. I shiver, crossing my arms. It's my fault my friend ended up here flat on his back. I doubt I can ever make this right. I clear my throat. "That's rough. I'm sorry to hear it."

Jack is pale and haggard. He squints at me, and my pulse races. I hope he won't recall what happened and how he hit his head. For the rest of my life, I'll be on edge, dreading a flicker of recognition in his eyes and the damning words naming me as the one who caused his traumatic brain injury.

I say, "I'm so sorry you're dealing with this, buddy."

Abby gives me a hug. "I'm glad you're here. Did you come up with the rest of money?"

I nod. "I'll tap my home equity line of credit. How much is needed? And by midnight tonight?"

Jack moans, and Abby says to him, "How can I help?"

He points to his head.

I cringe and pat Jack's cold hand. "We're here for you. Hang in there. It'll get better." I arch an eyebrow at the platitudes gushing from my mouth.

Abby pulls up the covers to his chin. "I'm sorry you're going through this, hon."

I grit my teeth at the damage I caused. Jack closes his eyes, and Abby says to me in a soft voice, "We've got to talk about the money."

23

ELGIN

I take an Uber from the hospital and wince as we go over bumps on the way to Millersville. What a hassle this assignment turned out to be. I thought it would be an easy job and take a day or two, but was I wrong. The driver drops me off at my car, which is parked near Jack's apartment. A parking ticket flutters under my windshield wiper, and I crumple it up, throwing it on the grass.

I slide into my car and moan. My right leg throbs, but the doctors didn't give me pain pills. Starting the engine, I clench my teeth as a zap of pain zings up my leg and through my body. Fishbone is the reason I was hurt. If he had paid Mother Mercy on time, I wouldn't have had to pay a visit to Millersville to hunt him down.

I head back to the hospital to see if his friends come up with the money by eleven. On the way, I notice a car tailing me two cars back. I take the next turn at Best Road and drive by farm fields, passing a sign advertising miniature donkeys. My plan is to buy five or ten acres with a cabin in the woods and maybe have a little donkey. That would be a sweet way to ride out the rest of my life. On days like this, when I'm wounded in my line of work, I'm ready to chuck it all and get out of this wretched business. The trouble is, I can't think of anything else that pays as well and calls for my skill set.

Last year when I told Mother Mercy I was thinking of quitting and living in the mountains, she said, "With all the jobs you've done for me and the things you know, I don't think you can quit." I've never met her in person, and she uses a machine that changes her voice on the phone, which creeps me out.

I glance in the rearview mirror and still see a car following me, so I pull off at a farm stand and wait for the car to pass. I open the glove compartment and pull out my gun. Rain drums down on my windshield.

A car pulls up behind me leaving the headlights on, shining in my rear-view mirror. A man with stooped shoulders gets out, and I exit my car and snort. What does an old fart with a long beard want?

24

JACKLYN

I put my hands on my hips and glance around my bungalow. I'm home after a haunting, harrowing stay at Shore Lodge, but I managed to come back to reclaim my dog and my home.

Buddy looks up at me and wags his tail. I say, "Irena and Kelly are in a tight spot. Let's take a walk and think of how to help them."

It is raining outside, so I leash my beagle-mix rescue dog and snap on the raincoat my friends Mary and Fred gave him. "You look handsome in orange," I tell him, and pull on my rain jacket. I step outside, and wind whips past my cheeks.

I wave to my neighbor, Bernard Frackus, a retired school teacher who is working at Gigi's Café. I admire him for washing dishes, bussing trays and ringing up orders with a smile. He's a good man, like my husband was. At times I find my mind and heart opening to the quiet possibility of meeting someone new, but they'd have to be good company.

The dog and I venture down the street in the driving rain, water splashing with each step. The wind howls, and I keep my head down, pondering my new venture with Stone Estates. I say to the dog, "I hope Albert would be proud of me for taking that on."

A hint of something negative nags at the back of my mind. I recently started a new business, but it might have been wise to wait before diving in and overseeing the construction of Stone Estates.

A neighbor pokes her head out of the garage. "Everything okay?"

I wave her off. "All good, thanks. Just chatting with my dog, like I always do."

She says, "Have a good night, then."

"You too."

The dog does his business, and we round the corner but stop in our tracks. A coyote watches us from fifteen yards away. Buddy's hackles rise. My heart pounds in my chest. Glancing around, I grab a stick and wave it in the air. "Go away."

The coyote stares with golden eyes, and my grip tightens on the stick. Buddy growls. I say to him, "Let's get out of here. We'll let the coyote have the corner tonight."

We turn around and hurry home, looking back every few steps. I unlock the door and rush inside, hanging up our coats. I towel Buddy off, and he shakes, water drops fly from his tail. I say, "I hope I haven't plunged in too deep. The permits are taking a long time to get."

The dog licks my cheek. I wrinkle my nose and examine the bottom of my boots. "Drat, I stepped in coyote scat. What a mess, which reminds me, Irena is raising money to help Jack. I'll call Bernice and Mary. We'll come up with something."

25

MERCURY

The car I'm following pulls off to the side of the road past a place selling miniature donkeys. A friend found Elgin Johnson's cell number and tracked his location. I've been on Johnson's tail since he picked up his car near Jack's apartment. I stop behind the sedan, letting my engine idle with the headlights on.

I climb out, and my hands clench. Johnson leans against the car with his right hand in his jacket pocket and says, "What do you want?"

"I want you to lay off Jack and his friends. Let them be."

He chuckles. "That's funny, but I can't do that. My job is to collect money from dead beats."

"At least give them until noon tomorrow," I say.

He cackles and pulls out a gun, aiming it at me. My stomach plummets at how foolish I was to follow him. I'm rusty at righteous antics and have no business being here by the road.

He says, "I'm calling the shots, long beard, and you're a nobody. Stay away from me, or you'll get hurt too."

I clear my throat. "What would make it worthwhile for you to leave town and forget Jack owed you money?"

"Nothing will. I'm not stopping." He cocks his head. "Why do you care so much? Who are you to Fishbone?"

He waves the gun at me, and my knees feel weak. My heart hammers in my chest. He could shoot me dead, roll me in a ditch, and no one would find me for days. By then, coyotes and crows would have had their fill of my flesh. I hold up my hands. "I'll tell you if you put the gun down."

He puts the gun in his pocket. Just then, my phone rings. "Go ahead," he says, "answer it. I bet it's the person who helped you tail me. They want to report that I've stopped and have been in the same position by the little donkeys for five minutes."

I answer the phone. Violet, who runs Outrigger Services, says, "Elgin Johnson has been in the same position for a few minutes. He's by the place selling donkeys. See if you can get to him there."

I say, "I'm talking with him right now."

"Excellent, any luck?" she says.

"Not yet."

She says, "Put me on speaker. I want to talk to him."

I put the phone on speaker and hold it up.

Violet says, "Elgin Johnson, aren't you supposed to be in jail right now?"

Johnson shakes his head. "I don't want to talk to your lady friend."

I say, "Why aren't you in jail? I heard you were hand-cuffed at the hospital."

He shrugs. "They let me go and said to show up for the court date. They have bigger problems to deal with."

I say, "There has to be something to get you off Jack's back."

He frowns. "Give me the money by eleven tonight. That'd do it. Back off, old man."

He gets in his car, and I consider hopping in mine and flooring it, rearending him. But that would accomplish nothing. Johnson drives away, extending his hand and giving me the middle finger.

I put the phone to my ear and say, "Violet, you still there?"

"I'm here. That didn't work, did it?"

I blow out a breath. "It didn't. What a waste of time. I could follow him, but I bet he's going to the hospital to harass Jack."

She says, "Abby has the nursing staff watching out for him, so Jack is safe for now. Come to the office, and we'll plot our next steps."

"See you soon."

I hang up and drive, musing about when I met Jack. I was looking out over the marina in Millersville and happened to see a young man sitting on a park bench with his head in his hands. His shoulders shook. I'd been alone and had rough times, so I went over and said, "Everything okay? Do you need help?"

He wiped his eyes. "I lost my job. The fifth one in six months."

"Mind if I sit down?"

He patted the green bench. "Go ahead. I've got nothing left to lose, except my wife and my baby girl."

I said, "What's the problem, do you think? Why do you keep losing jobs?"

He stared at a sailboat that was docking. "I can't concentrate. I lose track. And I'm not that interested in what I'm supposed to be doing."

I leaned back and nodded. "Some people luck out by landing jobs they love. Not many can be as lucky as that. Sounds like you're in the not-so-fun camp."

He sighed. "That's me, all right. I make mistakes, they realize I don't care about work, and then they can me."

We talked for a while and parted ways. But every now and then, we'd happen to be in the same area of the marina, and we'd sit and talk. That's how our friendship started, and it led to discussions he asked me not to tell his wife Irena about. We all carry secrets, and I'll keep his to my grave.

26

CRAIG

The small of my back hurts, and I curl up on a hard bunk in the jail cell, breathing through my mouth to avoid smelling pungent body odor permeating the air. I grit my teeth and think about how Jack ratted me out. Our marks were older people living alone, and we offered a supposed once-in-a-lifetime chance to double their money in six months. We didn't force people to sign up for our scheme. They were eager to throw money our way when their certificates of deposit matured.

My cell mate says from the lower bunk, "Tell me about the scam you were running, rich boy, to make the money you did. Tell me, or I'll hurt you again."

My eyes smart, and my gut is sore. He hit me in the stomach so hard that I almost passed out, and he said I was a low-life who scammed old people. When I get out of here, I'll straighten Jack out. I was an idiot to let him walk all over me.

A guard walks up to our cell and clears his throat. He says in a rumbling voice, "You on the upper bunk, it's your lucky day. Your parents posted bail, and you're getting out of here."

My cellmate stands, coughing in my face. I wince at the sour smell coming from his mouth and swing down from the upper bunk. My cellmate says, "So, the rich mama's boy is getting out. You owe me secrets about what you did, and I won't forget. When I get out, I'll look you up. You can tell me how to become a rich man."

My hands tremble, and I stand by the cell door, waiting for the guard to unlock it. The metal door opens, and I step out. The guard snaps on cuffs and glances at my face, where my cell mate hit me. He says, "Looks like you ran into a wall. Come on. We'll process you."

My cell mate says, "See you again."

I shudder and shuffle along. I can't wait to step outside, take a deep breath of fresh air and shake off my time in jail. When I'm home, I'll cook up a plan to get revenge. It's Jack's fault I was stuck in jail.

27

MERCURY

I stride up the steps to Outrigger Services and press the buzzer. Violet ushers me inside. She shows me into the bull pen and says to her crew, "This is Mercury Thunder, and he followed the cell phone you tracked. Let's gather round and come up with a plan for how to deal with Elgin Johnson."

Violet says, "These are my associates, Mimi and Flora. Vincent went home to help with his baby."

I flash a half-smile and hope they won't look into my background, because I moved to this small town to stay out of sight and start over. I shouldn't get involved, but I can't help it. Jack is a good guy, even though he has his troubles, and I'm like his long-lost uncle. I feel obligated to do what I can to protect him.

A few years back, Jack and I sat at the marina sipping coffee, looking over boats from a bench. He complained about not being able to hold down a job, and I said, "Want my opinion?" He nodded.

I said, "I'm not a doctor, but I think you show signs of having attention deficit disorder. You have trouble concentrating and following through on tasks, don't you?"

He said, "That's true."

I said, "You might look into it and mention it to a doctor."

But as far as I know, he never did. When I finish meeting at Outrigger Services, I'll go to the hospital and see how he is doing.

I grab a chair, and they move seats, forming a circle. Violet raps on the arm of her chair. "Okay, what do we know about this guy, Elgin Johnson?"

Mimi pulls her hair into a ponytail and says, "He collects on bad debts and works for an outfit called Mother Mercy, which might be a front for organized crime."

My eyebrows shoot up. "Did Jack borrow from the mob? I hope not."

Violet says, "We're not sure. We're digging into this Mother Mercy to find out who's behind it. Maybe we can get them to negotiate a settlement for less money."

Flora speaks up. Her voice has an edge to it when she says, "But isn't this Jack Fishbone's fault? He borrowed the money. Shouldn't he have to pay it back with interest like everyone else? Why are we so concerned about helping him?"

Violet says, "You're right, and I wouldn't do this for just anyone. I'm making an exception to my rule of not interfering in the consequences of stupid decisions for two reasons. Fishbone was hurt, possibly by people who loaned him money. And second, it's affecting his family, Irena, Abby, and his daughter, Kelly."

I clear my throat. "If ever there was an exception to be made, this is the moment. We've got a man in the hospital who doesn't know who he was. The thug coming after him just demanded more money at the last minute and moved up the deadline. I believe we have a righteous cause; do you agree?"

Violet, Mimi and Flora nod and say, "Yes."

Violet pushes up the sleeves of her gray sweatshirt. "Let's lay out a plan for who is doing what."

I stand and say, "If you don't mind, I want to visit Jack and see how he's doing."

Violet waves a hand. "Whatever you need to do is fine. We've got this. Just check in and tell us how Jack is doing, and if Abby and Irena can get the money by midnight, or if you see Elgin Johnson hanging out near or in the hospital."

I frown. "I heard the deadline was moved up from midnight. He wants more money by eleven tonight."

Violet glances at her phone. "That's in two and a half hours. That doesn't leave us much time."

I thank them and walk out the door, wiping my brow. Violet locks it behind me and draws the shade. I hurry down the stairs and think about Jack, the almost son I never had. He kept me in confidence as a secret confessor, and he didn't want me meeting his ex-wife or his new girl-friend. I guess we all need someone to tell secrets to without gossip spreading through town, and I was that person for Jack. But now it's time for me to step out of the shadows and meet the rest of the family.

28

FRANKIE

Frankie turned her chair in the FBI white-collar crime unit in Seattle and looked up at her boss. Alana frowned and said, "I guess you heard?"

Frankie nodded. "The guy running the scam on the elderly got out of jail. And our star witness doesn't remember anything."

Brick stood. "But he did recall one person's face, Abby Love. It's a sweet story, don't you think? And now they're married."

Frankie said, "Yes, it's a sweet story, but it doesn't get us anywhere."

Alana tugged on her ear lobe. "Talk to the new wife, see if she can shake anything out of Fishbone. Maybe she'll say something that will trigger his memory."

Frankie chewed on the inside of her mouth. "Let's take Fishbone to Martin Wharf and the cannery on the dead-end road. That might spark memories of when he hit his head."

Brick smiled, showing a dimple in his left cheek. "Good idea for a field trip."

"His condition is unstable, so it'll be a while," Frankie said, rubbing her temples.

Brick shrugged. "We'll be ready with a plan to jump start his memory."

Frankie's boss said, "This reenactment idea better pan out."

Crossing her arms, Frankie said, "Maybe he's blocking it out and doesn't want to remember."

Brick said, "Could be. We don't want the scam artist getting off on charges. He's saying Fishbone ran the entire operation."

"Fat chance of that," Frankie said. "Fishbone didn't strike me as having the brains to carry it out. Plus, the bulk of the money was transferred out of Fishbone's accounts."

Brick pushed back a lock of curly brown hair. "No way Fishbone ran it. He's out of money and couldn't pay his rent."

Frankie thumped a fist on her desk. "Fishbone's sneaker fetish got him into financial trouble. That's all he cared about."

Her boss cocked her head. "I wouldn't call collecting shoes a fetish, but more of a hobby. Take me for instance. I own thirty-two pairs of black pumps, but each pair is little different."

Brick said, "This isn't true in your case, but I'd say it verges on hoarding behavior. My great-aunt Melba hoarded toilet paper. When she passed away, my aunt found the second bedroom was filled with packages of toilet paper rolls."

Frankie arched an eyebrow. "So, that's where the toilet paper went during the pandemic."

The three chuckled and returned to the work of building an air tight case against Fishbone's friend, the scam artist.

29

MOTHER MERCY

The man who went by Mother Mercy wore a blue terry cloth bathrobe and sat on a brown leather recliner, scratching his armpit. He swallowed a slug of warm coffee and set the mug down on an end table. Shades were drawn in the living room and throughout the old two-story house. Caution was best, and he wasn't taking risks, not when he had a big pay day ahead. His man Elgin Johnson was going after the Fishbone fellow and bringing in what was owed with heavy surcharges for being overdue. You borrow, you pay it back, or you could go out in a casket. He'd explained that to Fishbone by phone, when the fool accepted the terms of the deal.

He shook his head at how Fishbone spent the borrowed money, by buying shoes. The pricey sneakers had been cleared out of the apartment, otherwise Mother

Mercy would have had Johnson grab the shoes and sell them to recoup some of the debt.

He pulled a cat treat out of his pocket and snapped his fingers. A black cat leaped onto his lap, took the treat, and ate it. Two parakeets fussed in a wire cage perched on a wooden stool by the closed window. The birds kicked bird seed out of the cage, and seeds fell on newspaper laid out over the carpet.

Mother Mercy said, "Cut that out. I know you want the curtains open, but I'm not doing it."

The cat meowed, birds tweeted, and Mother Mercy rubbed his sore stump. It was a crying shame doctors found gangrene in his right foot and cut it off. Phantom pain from his missing limb was no joke. If Fishbone thought his debt would be forgiven or forgotten because of life-threatening injuries, he was seriously mistaken. Mother Mercy wasn't going to cut Fishbone a break. Everyone had issues. Get real and deal with it.

He grabbed his crutches and thumped to the kitchen to brew a fresh pot of coffee. Glancing at a round wall clock, he furrowed his brow. Elgin Johnson was late calling with an update. Coffee dripped into the pot, and he drummed his fingers on the orange Formica counter top with a big, black burn mark. His bank account balance showed he had enough money to last beyond his lifetime, but he was smart enough not to flaunt it or flash it around.

He run a hand over his face and tugged a tissue from a box, dabbing his eyes. For reasons he didn't understand, his son refused to speak with him. No calls, no emails, no cards on birthdays or holidays. Randy lived somewhere in Southeast Asia and worked in digital communications, whatever that meant.

Mother Mercy shrugged. He did his best to raise his son as a single father, even if that meant leaving him at an overnight daycare when he was out of town. He had no choice, but the kid didn't see it.

The wall clock ticked, the second hand counting down until midnight. He pulled his phone from his bathrobe pocket and texted Johnson: 'Call to check in. What's the update?'

He poured a cup of coffee and slumped in a kitchen chair, staring out a streaked window into the backyard on a rainy night. His yellow 1972 Chrysler Newport sat in the driveway, lit by floodlights. He wished he could build a garage, but he didn't want people nosing around his place. It was bad enough suffering through the influx of new neighbors in their thirties. They renovated houses and smiled aggressively, asking how he was.

He scratched the back of his neck. Something didn't feel right, and in his line of work, listening to hunches made all the difference. Was Johnson pulling something behind his back? Maybe he increased the amount due and planned to skim off the top.

Mother Mercy sipped hot coffee and decided to cut Johnson from the payroll permanently after he finished the Fishbone job. Johnson was full of himself lately, which led to careless mistakes. The cat stalked into the kitchen and meowed, demanding a late snack. He said, "At least you're talking to me, which is more than I can say for my son."

He stood and opened the refrigerator, shivering in a blast of cold air, and pulled out a small container of fresh cat food. Shoving the door shut, he said, "Nothing but the best for my princess."

A knock at the back door made him flinch, dropping the cat food. The cat skittered away to hide under the kitchen table. Mother Mercy said, "Who could that be? I never have visitors."

30

———

ELGIN

I check my phone for the time and nod. I have a few hours before collecting the money or bashing in Fishbone's head. I might hurt him anyway if they pay up, as a penalty for the aggravation he caused. That would teach him a lesson.

"Siri," I say into my phone while driving with a hand on the wheel. "Find cabins for sale near me on five or ten acres in the mountains."

"Wait while I check." A moment later, Siri says, "I found one cabin for sale on five acres near you. Would you like directions to it?"

"Yes, but how much does it cost?"

"The price is one-hundred-fifty thousand dollars."

"Great. Take me there by the shortest route. I've got to see this place."

I drive and follow directions, turning off on a side road

and heading uphill. When the paved road gives way to a rutted dirt lane, I floor it and keep going. An hour passes, and I know I should turn back and go to the hospital to let Abby know I'll collect the cash in the parking lot. She hasn't called yet, which is odd considering the nurse gave her a note with my cell number. But the instinct to see this possibly gorgeous place of my dreams drives me forward, and I step on it. I bump along the dirt road, invested in the outcome, curious to see the cabin. It can't be far.

When I was growing up, my father always talked about when he hit the jackpot with the lottery or in a hold up, he'd buy a spread of land, and we'd live without a care in the world. He painted a vision of life away from people, in paradise in the mountains, with tall green trees surrounding a one-bedroom cabin. I smile, recalling how he said we'd be safe there, and no one would force me to go to school.

With a jolt, the car skids to a stop on the primitive, rutted one-lane road. I open the door and climb out, staring out into a dark abyss. A coyote howls, and hairs stand on end on my arms. My car is high-centered, and I can't leave here without help. I slap my forehead, angry at my stupidity for getting stuck in the middle of nowhere. I was a fool to rush up here when I have business to do in town, and I learned the road to paradise isn't paved.

I gingerly ease into the car, dragging my sore leg, and pick up my phone. I press a button and say, "Siri, call a tow truck."

Silence.

I clench my jaw and work the phone, trying to search online for towing companies, but it doesn't have a signal. I noticed the navigation directions quit about five miles back, but I assumed when I turned a corner and moved out of the dense forest, I'd get reception. No luck tonight.

My body trembles with rage. Letting out a roar, I stumble from the car, ignoring the piercing pain in my right thigh, and I fling the phone out into the darkness. It sails into the air. On its way down, a voice says, "Would you like to place a call?"

I put my hands on my knees and yell, "Siri, call a tow truck company. Get me out of this mess."

My voice echoes. I'm alone in a vast forest, with no one coming to help. What have I done to myself?

Lightning cracks in the distance, thunder rumbles and hairs stand on end on the back of my neck. Rain pours down, plastering my hair against my head, forming puddles at my feet and getting my shoes wet. Throwing my arms out, I scream into the night.

31

MERCURY

I park at the hospital and hurry through the lot. A small group of women march outside the building, holding protest signs that say, 'Donate to Help Jack Fishbone.' A sign held by a blue-eyed lantern-jawed woman in her sixties says: 'We've got your back, Jack.' She's wearing hiking boots with mismatched socks and khaki shorts, which strikes me as an interesting choice of attire.

I nod to the blue-eyed woman and say, "You're right, we need to help Jack."

She smiles. "Tell your friends. And I'm Jacklyn, Jacklyn Stone, by the way." She extends a hand, and we shake.

"I'm Mercury Thunder."

Her hand is warm on a cool, damp night, and rain

drizzles down, leaving mist in the air. She steps back, and I say, "Nice to meet you."

I open the door and consider my brief encounter. When I moved to Millersville, I agreed to keep a low profile and not mention my past. But how much risk would it pose to get to know a woman about my age with sparkling blue eyes?

I head down a stark hall to reception and wonder what I'll find when I get to Jack's room. A young woman with tattooed arms at the desk gives me his room number, and I take the elevator, mulling over the last time we spoke. Jack was wrestling with his habit of buying shoes, and he realized borrowing money squashed his self-esteem. He also talked about how he was keeping secrets from his friend Craig, who was running a scam.

I step off the elevator on the eighth floor and smile. The woman outside with blue eyes didn't look like she would suffer fools. Maybe when this situation blows over, I'll find her and ask her out for coffee.

JACK

An older man with a long pointed gray beard enters my room, and Abby lets go of my hand. She stands and says, "Hello, who are you?"

He tugs on his mustache. "I'm a friend of Jack's. We go a long ways back. My name is Mercury Thunder."

Abby puts her hands on her hips. "He hasn't mentioned you, and I know his friends. Are you a reporter?"

The man holds up his hands and takes a step back. He's wearing orange sneakers with a white waffle sole. His blue raincoat drips on the floor. He says, "I'm sorry if I alarmed you. I'm not a reporter. Jack, don't you remember me?"

I shake my head and eye the red bowtie attached to his beard below his chin.

He runs his long fingers over his face and wipes a tear

from his eyes. "I'm sorry for barging in. I was just worried about him. Please forgive me, and I hope we'll meet on better terms when Jack regains his memory."

Abby swallows and says, "But we don't know if he'll get his memory back."

The bearded man pulls out a business card, giving it to her. "Call me, if there's anything I can do to help. Jack and I met at the marina years ago, and we've been meeting for coffee there on and off ever since."

She says in a low voice, "He has a long road ahead. If he survives the night and we keep the debt collector away, he'll have to learn to walk, talk and eat."

The man's shoulders sink, and he leans against the wall. "We've got to keep him safe. I'll tell everyone I know to donate to the fundraiser."

A nurse comes in and says, "Are you family?"

The man tugs on his mustache. "I'm not, but I felt like I was before this."

The nurse touches the frames of her glasses. "I'm sorry, but you'll have to leave."

He says to Abby, "It was nice to meet you. Jack told me a lot about you and how much he cared for you, and I can see why. Goodbye." He waves to me and walks away.

The nurse takes my vitals, and Abby says to me, "Sorry about that. I'll do a better job of filtering people and fending off odd balls from now on."

32

ELGIN

I scream, and my voice echoes off a cliff. Cold wind whistles past, making trees sway, and a shiver runs through me. Rubbing my arms, I flinch when a branch nearby falls to the ground with a thud.

I drag my bad leg and stumble on the dirt track. My ankle twists, and I bellow at my stupidity. I never should have come up here. Now, I'll be late going to collect the money.

A twig snaps, and I tense, looking around. My pulse pounds in my ears. To my right, tall trees close in, and the quiet in the woods makes me nervous. Someone or something could be watching, poised to attack.

I release a shallow breath and shake out my hands to release tension. It's probably just a deer, not a hungry black bear. But then I picture a bobcat eyeing me, ready to jump, and my stomach knots.

I shuffle to the car, climb in with a groan and break down sobbing. I'm late to check in with my boss, and I have no way to get out of here. A crunching sound in the backseat startles me, and I whip my head around. A large raccoon stares at me, with a paw in a bag of potato chips. I yelp and propel myself out of the car. In my hurry, I stumble and fall off the edge of the road, screaming on the way down.

MOTHER MERCY

Mother Mercy tightened his bathrobe tie, grabbed his crutches and made his way to the back door. A blond woman in her thirties stood on the porch holding a plate covered with tin foil. She rapped on the door three times, and he called, "Coming."

He patted down his hair and swung open the door. She was wearing bright yellow workout gear. Mother Mercy winced, reminded of how Elgin Johnson, who was late calling to check in, despised the color yellow. He couldn't recall the name for that phobia, but there was one, Johnson had told him with pride.

He gazed at his visitor and said, "Hello, you must be one of my new neighbors."

She smiled and pushed a platter toward him. "I brought over some food for you."

He pointed to his crutches. "Leave it on the steps. I'll get it later."

"Oh, it's no problem, I'll bring it in." She pushed her way past him and stood in the kitchen, looking around. Her jaw fell open. "This is an amazing kitchen. I like what you've got going on here. Who was your designer?"

He left the door open, hoping she'd get the hint and leave. "The designer has been dead a long time. My mother picked it out."

She glanced at the spotless counter. "Shall I put the platter here?"

He shrugged. "Sure, fine. Very thoughtful of you. What is it?"

She tapped a finger to her lips and peered into the living room, but he stumped over to block the doorway with his body. No one went in his inner sanctuary, where his business was set up. Birds chirped, as if asking about the stranger.

She stood on her tiptoes looking over his shoulder, standing too close. Invading his space would have meant sudden death for her ten years ago, but he had mellowed with age. He gestured to the door with his chin and hoped she would leave.

She stepped over to the white gas range. His mother had loved the griddle on top in the middle, where she cooked pancakes on Saturdays and stacked them on a plate for him in the warming oven. He would come downstairs sleepy-eyed, inhaling the comforting smells of a weekend morning. The oven could fit a twenty-two-pound turkey, his mother said with a smile, but that was before his father left. Thanksgivings were a dour affair after he found another woman in the next town. From then on, his mother put on a nurse's uniform, complete with a starched white hat, which she never took off except when going to bed. She got a job as a nurse's aide at a nursing home nearby and announced she would only speak to her son from seven until eight o'clock each evening. That's when his dark times started.

His unwelcome, unwanted visitor clapped her hands, bringing him back to the present. She beamed and said, "I brought shrimp enchiladas, crab cakes, sugar snap peas and extra tartar sauce. I made it myself."

He cleared his throat. "You'd best take it home. I'm allergic to shellfish."

She squinted, looking up at him. "What happens if you eat it?"

"My lips, tongue and throat swell. I have trouble breathing. I could die."

Her eyes grew wide. "In that case, I'll just leave the peas. If I knew your food preferences beforehand, I wouldn't have made this mistake." She flashed him an accusing look, like it was his fault.

"Well, you're new to the neighborhood," he said in his defense.

She frowned. "We've lived next door for three years. You never leave your house, so you don't see us."

He forced out a fake chuckle. "I'm not one to mix with others. I keep to my work."

She tilted her head and crossed her arms. "What is your line of work?"

"A little of this and a little of that. Now, if you'll be so kind as to take your plate of food, I'll close the door, so the cat won't get out."

She looked around, and for the life of him, he couldn't remember her name. She came over with her husband and rang the doorbell when they moved in, but their names washed over him, sounding the same. Jessica and James maybe. Jennifer and Justin. It was a blur. There were only two people he wanted to hear from, Elgin and his son.

He moved to the door and opened it a few more inches. He said, "Watch out for the cat. I wouldn't want you to trip, take a tumble and hurt yourself on the steps." He chewed on the inside of his mouth and suppressed a partial smile as pleasant memories from the past roared back when his client, who owed far more than the Fishbone fellow, met her final end in part because of her haughty attitude. She had insisted she did not need to pay Mother Mercy back. But he had straightened her out and had the last word.

His perky, pesky neighbor hefted the platter and turned to the door, but the cat dashed outside. He grabbed a handful of cat treats and started to hurry out to coax the cat inside, but the visitor bumped into him with her hip, knocking him off balance.

He yelled as he fell down the steps, and Johnson's face came to mind. Why hadn't he called? Mother Mercy smacked into the pavement below to the sound of bones cracking. He clenched his jaw, vowing not to let a whimper of pain escape his lips.

She bent over him, giving off an eye-watering odor of floral scented dryer sheets, making him sneeze. "Are you all right?" she said.

"What does it look like? I think my leg is broken, maybe my arm too. Call an ambulance."

33

ABBY

I hold Jack's hand until he falls asleep and step to the window to call Irena. When she picks up, I say in a quiet voice, "How much money do we have now?"

She says, "Mercury Thunder chipped in ten thousand dollars because he said Jack is like the son he never had. But we're still short of what we need."

I cringe, thinking of how harsh I was with the older man who came to see Jack. "Are we talking about the guy with a long gray beard?"

"Yes."

"I should've been nicer to him. I doubted he knew Jack."

Irena starts to say something, but my attention is diverted when someone raps hard on the door. A man says in a booming voice, "Is Jack here? I've come to settle grievances with my friend."

I eye Craig as he marches in. His face is red and raw, like someone beat him up. I whisper into the phone, "I have to go. Craig's here."

"Craig? I thought he was in jail."

"Got to go," I say, hanging up on her. I stand between Craig, who is bearing down on Jack, and my husband, who is waking up. Extending my arms, I say to Craig, "Keep your voice down. He needs to rest, so he can recover. Aren't you supposed to be in jail?"

He grins, featuring a crooked incisor. "My folks bailed me out." He turns to Jack and says in a loud voice, "Thanks a lot, buddy. You turned me in, and because of you, I spent time in jail. You owe me for that."

I say, "Keep your voice down and stop threatening him. He has a brain injury."

Jack points to Craig and then at his own head.

I rush to his side and a dawning realization sweeps over me. I hold his hand and say, "Did Craig cause your head injury?"

Jack nods and winces. His fingers squeeze my hand.

I say, "I understand." He relaxes his hand. I turn to Craig and glare at him, saying, "You hit him and left him at the wharf? How could you?"

Jack moans, touching his forehead.

Craig shoves his hands in the pockets of his khaki pants and looks down at the floor. "I don't know what you're talking about."

I say, "Jack, squeeze my hand if he's the one who did it."

He squeezes my fingers.

I stride over to Craig. "Shame on you for coming here and for what you did. You'd better leave, or I'll call security. They'll escort you from the building and right back to jail."

Craig holds up his hands. "I swear I didn't hurt Jack. I wanted to, but I didn't. I had nothing to do with what happened that put him here. And you better think seriously before accusing me, because I know a good attorney. I'd never stoop that low to harm a friend. You're crazy to think that."

But from the way he doesn't meet my gaze, scuffs a toe and stares at the window as he speaks, I doubt his sincerity. I stare at the near-killer who was our friend and glower. We all knew Craig had a mean streak, but I never thought he'd come close to killing Jack.

Craig backs up to the wall and points at Jack. "I didn't do this, but there'll be payback for what you did, turning me into the authorities."

He strides out, and a doctor wearing a white lab coat comes in. Her black hair is pulled back, and her white name tag with black letters shows: 'Dr. Wang.'

She says, "I'm here to check on you. Let's see how you're doing."

34

JACK

Dr. Wang asks how I'm feeling, and I open my hands, giving a slight shrug. My skull feels like a pickaxe hit it, there's a tube sticking out my throat and this Craig person coming in radiating anger didn't help. I'm stuck in a broken body, and my mood has taken a nasty nose dive.

I try to say something but words don't come out.

Abby says, "I think he's frustrated he has a tube in his throat. He wants to talk."

Dr. Wang holds up a small device in a clear plastic bag. "We want you to rest now, but tomorrow you can try covering the trach tube with your finger to talk. We'll attach a speaking valve like this one tomorrow. It'll go on the outside of the tracheostomy tube, and a nurse will monitor you while you use it."

I cringe and look at Abby, who pats my arm and says

to the doctor, "Thanks, we appreciate your update. I'm sure he's looking forward to being able to talk."

Dr. Wang nods and says to me, "The speaking valve should help you swallow and manage secretions. We may have to suction the tube before placing the valve."

I wrinkle my nose and wince to indicate my displeasure. Suctioning secretions sounds disgusting. A tear trickles down my cheek. I feel as though I'm a failure, not giving Abby the husband she deserves.

When the doctor leaves, Abby perches on the bed. "We knew it wouldn't be easy, didn't we?"

I give a slight nod.

She says, "We've been friends for many years, and we know each other very well. Right?"

I arch an eyebrow in response.

She says, "I know you're tough, and you can do this. You're strong and loving and a good man. Hang in there. You're going to walk out of the hospital in no time."

I bite my lower lip, hoping she's right.

Someone knocks, and a tall Black man in his forties wearing tortoise shell framed glasses, a white lab coat and blue scrubs comes in. Abby slides off the bed and stands by me.

"I'm Dr. Rhodes. How are you feeling?"

I tilt my head and open my hands to show I'm kind of okay, considering the circumstances. A sudden jolt of pain pierces my skull, and I wince, touching my forehead.

He says, "I'd like to look at your head to see if the swelling has gone down."

He steps out to the hall and returns with a nurse. He washes his hands and pulls on a fresh pair of blue disposable gloves. He says, "We're going to take off the bandages."

He unwraps the bandages, and I frown. I really don't want to undergo another surgery. I want the pain to vanish, I want the piece of my skull put back, and I want the tube removed from my neck.

I watch Abby to see if she shows signs of disgust as bandages come off my head. She swallows and takes my hand, looking into my eyes. "Everything will be fine. You'll get through this. I'm here for you."

Dr. Rhodes says something in a low voice to the nurse and clears his throat. My hands clench, and I hold my breath, waiting for the news. He says, "I'm pleased to say the swelling has gone down. We'll keep an eye on it."

The doctor and nurse apply fresh bandages. Abby says, "Thank you, Dr. Rhodes for saving his life and operating on him."

He flashes a shy smile and shrugs. "It's what we do."

When they leave, Abby turns to me and kisses my cheek. "They're taking good care of you."

I smile and close my eyes, letting my mind wander and basking in the good news about my brain. I wonder if I'd like to be a nurse's assistant or a nurse when I recover. I don't know how much training is involved for each path. I cast my mind back to my school years and realize I have no idea if I got good grades or had a hard time concentrating.

Abby squeezes my hand and whispers in my ear, "We'll meet the challenges ahead, my love. We'll take small steps at a time, and we'll get there."

She releases my hand and steps away. I open my eyes. She picks up her purse and says, "I'm going to the cafeteria. I won't be long."

She walks out, closing the door quietly. I lean back on the pillow and let pent up tears run down my face. I want to stay alive and leave the hospital and chew and swallow food. Those goals feel as challenging as climbing a mountain, and I have a good chance of making it.

35

____

BUZZ

I stop at the bookstore to check our sales for the day, and the shop is closed, so I stand outside the door, digging in my jeans pocket for keys. My fingers touch a piece of paper, and I pull out the note a nurse asked me to give Abby. My face heats, and I fumble with my keys, unlock the door and call Abby as I rush to my office.

She picks up, and I say, "Abs, I'm sorry, but I found something important I should've given you. Can you talk now, or are you with Jack?"

"I'm in the cafeteria trying to buy sushi, but I can't figure out how to use the machine to pay for it."

A woman in the background says, "Let me help you. The machines are touchy at times."

"Hold on," Abby says. "This'll take a minute."

I run a hand through my hair and frown at papers

strewn over my desk. Everything has been in disarray since I hit Jack by the cannery. I'm tense and worried, waiting to be caught and locked up. My right eye twitches as I glance at the wall clock and shake my head. It is approaching nine p.m., and I need to go home to walk my dog.

Rain patters on the window panes, and I chew on my lower lip. Should I confess and turn myself in? I could be put in prison for attempted second degree murder. I clench my jaw, reliving what happened at the wharf that night. We said goodbye on the dead-end dirt road, and Jack pulled out a new burner phone, saying he was going to call Irena and take her, Kelly and his secret girlfriend into what sounded like witness protection. That meant I'd never see Irena again. Before I knew it, my fist flew at his head in a flood of panicked rage.

Abby comes back on the line. "Okay, what's up?"

"I'm sorry, but a nurse gave me a note to give to you."

"Buzz, it sounds important. How could you forget to tell me this?"

I swallow, and my ears click. "I'm sorry. I've had a ton on my mind."

She sighs. "You're not alone in that. What does it say? Read it to me."

I read it aloud, and she gasps. She says, "Elgin Johnson left that so I could call and arrange to pay the money. Read that phone number again, will you?"

I repeat the number, and she says in a breathless voice, "Got to go. Bye."

I hang up and blow out a breath. I'm an utter failure and only good at fouling up relationships lately. I groan and run my hands down my face. What have I done?

Someone clomps in the store, and a man says in a loud voice, "Hello?"

I wipe away tears with the back of my hand and step out of my office. In my haste coming in, I forgot to lock the door behind me. A gray-haired man with a weather-worn face pushes back a cowboy hat and says, "The door was open, so I figured it was okay to come in."

"We're closed," I say. "We open at eight tomorrow morning."

"I'm not here to buy books. I'm looking for a woman named Irena Pickle. She'd be about forty by now. Have you seen her around? I think she lives in Millersville."

I put my hands on my hips and say, "Who are you and why are you asking?"

He shifts his feet. "I'm interested in finding her. No need to go into why."

I cock my head and consider what to say. This man might be Irena's father, but she didn't want to have any contact with him. I need to find out who he is without divulging she lives in town. Her dad was locked up in jail on the east side of the mountains for killing a man in a bar fight, but he might have been released on parole.

I scratch my ear. "I'm just closing up. Why don't you

tell me what your name is, and why you're looking for that woman."

His jaw clenches, and a vein pulses in his forehead. He shoves a hand in his pocket and says, "You might want to be more polite to strangers like me who are new to town. Now let's start over, shall we?"

I play a hunch and say, "Are you Irena's father?"

He grins, showing a gap from a missing tooth in front. There's something menacing in his smile, and his dark eyes squint at me. The tick in my eye intensifies. I want to get him out of here, so we're not alone in a standoff.

He says, "Sounds like you know my daughter."

Irena told me she wanted nothing to do with him. When she was young, her father was short-tempered and hit her mother. Her dad went to prison, and her mother took her over the mountains to live in our small water-front town, leaving no forwarding address.

I rub my chin. I want him to leave, and I don't want to discuss what I know about his daughter. I have to get home to let my dog out, and Irena and Abby need my help dealing with the debacle devised by the debt collector. I say, "Let's step outside."

He glances out the door at rain coming down. "Tell me what I need to know now."

I take a deep breath and consider what to say that will keep Irena safe.

ELGIN

I cringe when coyotes yip, snarl and growl close by. Hairs on my arms stand on end. The sounds are menacing, as if circling for a kill. Cold night air cuts through the thin shirt I'm wearing, and I shiver, crossing my arms for warmth. I bend my knees and hobble the few steps back to the road.

The coyotes are suddenly silent, and my eyes dart around in the dark. I hope the creatures aren't sneaking up on me. Glancing up the hill, I see a tall man striding down the rutted dirt track toward me, carrying something. It could be a tree branch, a baseball bat or a rifle in his hand. Light from the crescent moon shines, but I can't make out his features or the expression on his face.

I frown, because I'm normally a tough guy, but not tonight. I'm having trouble walking, my leg is throbbing with pain, and I just want to get back to Mt. Vernon and grab a cup of hot coffee. My idea to explore the wilds on a whim was one of my more stupid ones, topped only by the time I married a waitress I had met three days before.

Coyotes break into frenzied barking, making hairs on the back of my neck stand on end. My hands tremble, and rain runs down my face.

The man points in the direction of the coyotes and says, "Quiet."

I breathe a sigh of relief at the sudden silence and grimace when it occurs to me that I'm trapped out here. I could die tonight at the hands of a stranger. Taking a breath of cool forest air, I clear my throat. "Can you help me? My car is stuck."

The man strides closer and doesn't reply. It looks like a rifle in his hand. I'm a big, broad-shouldered guy, but with this mountain man, I've more than met my match.

My throat goes dry, and my stomach sours. I point to my car and say, "Can you help me get out of here?"

He stops, raising the gun to his shoulder.

I'm in deep trouble.

36

BUZZ

I cock my head, eying the man who said he's Irena's father. Whether she sees him or not should be her decision. "I don't think she wants to see you, but I'll call her and see if she's changed her mind."

I dial Irena, and she picks up on the second ring. Before I can say anything, she says, "Buzz, we need you to use your line of credit to help Jack. Are you still willing to do that?"

I clear my throat. "Sure, I can do that, but it's not why I'm calling. You father is here in my store, and he's asking about you."

She's silent for beat before quietly saying, "But he was in prison. Why is he here? We didn't tell him where we moved."

I cover the phone and say to him, "She wants to know why you want to see her after all this time?"

He marches over, grabs the phone from my hands and says, "Hey sweet girl, it's been a long time, and I want to get to know you after all these years. Where do you live? I'd like to stop over and see you."

She says something in a loud voice, and he holds the phone out to me, saying, "Guess that didn't go like I pictured it. She wants to talk to you."

I hold the phone to my ear and say, "Irena?"

She says in a low voice, "Don't tell him where I live or work, whatever you do. I don't want to talk to him. I don't want to see him. The way he treated my mom was beyond horrible. I won't expose Kelly to his unpredictable mood swings and anger."

She hangs up, and I'm left standing in a dark bookstore with a murderer who wants to find my former girlfriend. "Sorry," I say, "sounds like she's made up her mind not to see you. I've got to lock up now."

"See you around," he says, tipping his hat and stepping out in the rain. He lumbers over to a gray four-door older model sedan and climbs in, closing the door.

I breathe out a sigh of relief, pull on my rain coat and shut the bookstore door, locking it and checking it twice. The gray sedan idles nearby. I hurry through the rain to my car and climb in, closing and locking the door. On the way home, I glance in the rear-view mirror but don't see anyone following me. As I pull into my carport and get out, the gray sedan comes around the corner and stops, engine idling, across the street. Irena's father leans over the steering wheel and watches me as I enter my house.

A chill runs up my spine. I could be in danger, but my dog still needs to go out, despite the rain and Irena's father. I ruffle my dog's ears, leash him up and we go out, walking five blocks like we always do. I hurry ahead, stepping in puddles and not caring, and my dog matches me step for step. He bends to do his business, and I dutifully pick it up. I frown as we hurry home, because there's not much time left to access my line of credit and get the money to Abby.

We approach the house, and my dog growls. Standing on my front porch under the overhang, sheltered from rain, is Irena's father. I don't have time to talk to him, and I don't want to invite him in.

He takes off his cowboy hat and holds it on his chest. "Small towns are known to be friendly places. Thought I'd invite myself in, seeing as you're a friend of my daughter's."

I shake my head, and the dog sniffs his boots. "This isn't a good time. Got a lot going on tonight."

He steps between me and the door and swipes the house keys from my hand. He says, "Let me rephrase my statement. You're going to invite me in, give me a hot cup of coffee and answer my questions. Aren't you?"

I grab the keys back and point to his car. "No, that's not how this is going to go. Get in your car now or I'll sic my dog on you."

Happy growls, showing his teeth and straining on the leash.

The man inches away with his hands in the air. "I know where you live, and I'll be back. I'll find Irena without your help." He stomps to his car, splashing through a deep puddle and cursing.

I'm sweating as I unlock the door with shaking hands. When we're safe inside, I close the door and slam the deadbolt home. "Thanks for protecting me out there. How about a treat?"

We race to the pantry, where I pull out a pumpkin dog treat. I tell him to sit and toss him the treat. If only dealing with humans was as easy as training a dog.

A car starts, and the engine revs. I glance out the living room window and watch the gray sedan race away, tires spinning on the wet pavement. Rain drips off the gutters, and a feeling of dread sweeps over me. If only Irena had agreed to meet with him, I wouldn't be taking the brunt of his anger.

I feed the dog, towel him down, and grab a quick bite to eat while I check my home equity line of credit. My jaw drops because a message on bank's website says, "Service down for maintenance. Check back in 24 hours."

37

ABBY

I call Elgin Johnson, but he doesn't pick up and his voice mailbox is full. When I call Irena, she says, "I think we found the way to pay Jack's debt to this Mother Mercy person."

I stare out the window at the river, where workers are placing sand bags to prevent flooding from recent rain storms. "How?"

"Buzz will tap his home equity line of credit, which means we're all set. Isn't that great news?"

I say, "I wish it were that simple, but I can't reach Elgin Johnson. He was discharged from the hospital, and I don't know where he is, so I can't give him the money. He's not answering his phone. I wish I knew how to reach this Mother Mercy person directly."

"That's horrible. Hold on, Buzz is calling. I'll call you

after I tell him how much to transfer. He doesn't know the amount yet."

I stand at the window, hot air blowing from a vent at my knees. Jack is sleeping, and he looks ten or fifteen years older. I kiss his stubbled cheek and whisper, "I'm so glad you're alive. If I hadn't found you, my heart would've been broken. I love you, Jack."

His eyelids flutter, and I pat his hand. I flinch when the phone rings and quickly answer it, so as not to wake Jack.

Irena says, "Buzz can't get the money until tomorrow night. What'll we do?"

I step away from the bed and say in a low voice, "You two focus on crowd funding and selling Jack's shoes. I'll keep trying to reach him to negotiate what we owe. Maybe I can find this Mother Mercy person."

Irena laughs. "Fat chance with that. It must be a front for a mob operation, where they lend money under a fake name. No one goes by that name."

She hangs up, and I pull out my laptop to search for the boss of the operation. It might be foolish to attempt to reach Johnson's superior, but he isn't answering his phone. Maybe his boss would say it's okay to pay part of what we owe by midnight, and the rest in a week. I roll my eyes and tap on my keyboard. One can hope.

38

MOTHER MERCY

Sirens wailed in the distance. Mother Mercy lay on the ground, his leg and arms sticking out at odd angles. Neighbors crowded around as pain pulsed through his body, and every nerve was on alert. Toes on his phantom missing foot tingled, followed by a zap of pain, making him moan.

The pushy neighbor who barged in hovered over him on her knees, pushing her pointed nose in his face. He turned his head away and coughed, so she'd get the hint, but she moved closer. He couldn't wait to get away from her. His cat was the only creature he let get close.

Speak of the devil, The Cat came over and rubbed against him, purring. Mother Mercy said, "Someone take my cat inside and lock the door, will you?"

Justin or Jason or Jeremy, the husband of the intruding

neighbor, scooped up the cat, startling it. The cat clawed his face, leaving long red scratches, and he dropped it, issuing a slew of swear words. The cat ran off.

Mother Mercy moaned. His new neighbors had made an art of helping into a hindrance. They were clumsy, wrong-way motivated with misguided intentions. When he got home from the hospital, he planned to keep his door locked and never speak to these dull-witted young neighbors again.

An ambulance pulled up, cutting the sound of a wailing siren. He attempted to sit up but couldn't. He stayed on his back staring into the night sky, rain hitting his face.

"Move aside," a woman said in a commanding voice. "Make way."

Two people in dark blue uniforms set down a stretcher beside him. A man in his forties took his blood pressure. The woman said, "Can you tell me what happened?"

He grimaced and squinted at the offending party, his overly-perky neighbor. He was about to throw her under the bus but decided, for the sake of maintaining a civil relationship with his neighbors, not to accuse her of knocking him down the steps, which she clearly did. He cleared his throat and said, "The cat ran out, and I fell down the steps."

The female EMT checked his pupils, shining a flashlight in his eyes. "Can you tell me what hurts?"

He said, "Everything, especially my right leg and foot."

She looked at her partner, and they exchanged a quick glance. Mother Mercy said, "I know they cut off my leg below the knee, but the pain in that limb is still killing me. Other than that, I think my other leg might be broken, maybe my arm too."

They checked his limbs. The female EMT stood up and put her hands on her hips. "We're taking you to the hospital. Tacoma General is closest."

He groaned. "Great, and then I get to wait in the ER for hours along with everyone else."

She said, "Are you diabetic?"

He nodded. "Been that way for years."

"We'll bring you in, and we might be able to move you into an exam room to wait to see a doctor."

He sighed. "Just take me away, and let's get this fixed. I have business to attend to back at home."

He called out in the direction of Justin Jason and his wife Jennifer Jessica, "Please feed my cat, but don't go inside my house."

Jennifer Jessica said, "The cat just went in, and I shut the door."

He blew out a breath. "Good, make sure the door is locked. I'll be back soon."

"We will," her husband said, waving goodbye as the attendants hauled him away on a stretcher. "Don't worry, everything will be just fine while you're gone."

Something about the way he wouldn't meet Mother

Mercy's eyes made him doubt the man's sincerity. His chest tightened with fear. The worst thing would be if his neighbors took advantage of his being gone by going inside and being doubly nosy.

He said, "Lock the door while I'm gone."

The neighbor said, "We will. Don't worry about a thing."

"Get well," Jennifer Jessica said in her grating high-pitched voice.

Mother Mercy frowned as they lifted him, loading him into the aid car. If she hadn't been in his house, he never would have fallen at a critical time for his business. He patted his pockets and found a few cat treats. "My phone," he said. "I need my phone."

"Hold on," the female EMT said. "I'll look for it and be right back. I won't be long."

A few minutes later, she stepped into the back of the aid car and closed the doors. She shook her head. "Sorry, I couldn't find it."

He said, "Did you look in the yard? It must've fallen out of my pocket."

She held up her hands. "I looked everywhere. No luck."

She strapped into a seat and thumped on the wall behind the driver, calling, "Okay, let's go."

As the vehicle moved ahead, Mother Mercy examined the ceiling of the aid car and felt his vice-like grip on his carefully controlled life start to disintegrate. When he got home, he might devise a delicate way to end the cheery neighbor woman's life in a secretive manner as payback for this debacle. And his house had better be the way he left it when he arrived back home or there will be trouble in Tacoma.

39

FRANKIE

Frankie's phone rang, and she answered out of habit, although it was nine in the evening. In her line of work, she was always on call. White collar criminals didn't keep only day time hours. They were nocturnal as well, like varmints.

A woman on the line said, "Special Agent McNalley? I'm Abby Love, and I'm calling about the man who broke into Jack Fishbone's apartment and choked me."

Frankie nodded. "Sure, I remember you. We spoke in the hospital. What's going on?"

Abby said, "That man has been after Jack to pay an overdue loan. We were to pay him a certain amount tonight, but he's not answering his phone, and he left the hospital. I'm worried because he said if we didn't pay by a certain time, he'd hurt Jack."

Frankie paused the show she was watching and said,

"Are you saying you're looking for Elgin Johnson to pay him back, so nothing happens to your husband?"

"Yes, and I'm calling to see if you know who Mother Mercy is, Johnson's boss. I can't find her online, and I thought you might know who she is, so I can call and ask to put off making the payment. We need more time. We don't have the money."

Frankie rolled her eyes and couldn't resist saying, "All of this trouble because of sneakers. It beats me how someone could make footwear that important."

Abby sighed. "I know what you mean, but the deadline is eleven tonight, and I don't want Johnson showing up to hurt Jack."

"My partner and I looked into Mother Mercy and didn't find much. But we'll see if we can dig up anything else, given the time constraint."

"One more thing before you go," Abby said. "Jack identified Craig as the person who hurt his head and left him for dead."

Frankie's pulse picked up. She said, "That's important to know. I've got to go." She hung up and dialed Special Agent Mark Brick, who answered on the first ring with music blaring in the background. He said in a loud voice, "Good evening, Special Agent McNalley. How may I help you?" The music grew quiet.

She smiled. "Knock it off, Brick. I just got a call from Fishbone's new wife, Abby Love. She said Elgin Johnson is in the wind and threatened to hurt Fishbone if he and his friends don't pay back the debt to Mother Mercy by eleven tonight. And, get this, she mentioned Fishbone fingered his buddy Craig as the guy who caused his brain trauma. We'll add that to our list of charges. Maybe we can get the judge to set the bail higher and bring him back in before he hurts Fishbone again."

Brick said, "We can't let Fishbone get hurt. We need him alive and well to testify at the trial. Maybe this is the start of his memory coming back."

She nodded. "That's what I was thinking. I hope so. Fishbone's wife asked for a way to contact Mother Mercy, Johnson's boss, to negotiate a later payment. They don't have the money to pay it back by the deadline tonight."

He said, "Fishbone is our witness, so we've got to protect him until the trial ends. But we came up with a big nothing on Mother Mercy, didn't we?"

"We did. But what about the LLC registered to a man in Tacoma? It was called Mercy Limited. It's a stretch, but maybe that's where Elgin Johnson's boss is located."

"Want to take a ride and check it out? Nothing like banging on a door at night for fun."

She said, "Sure thing, let's go. I'll tell the boss what's going on, and we'll send someone to guard Fishbone at the hospital. The list of charges against the scam artist just got longer, and we're dead-serious about taking him down."

40

ELGIN

I shudder and eye a tall man pointing a rifle at me. He says in a booming voice, "Who are you and why are you trespassing on our land?"

My throat grows tight. "I'm sorry, I didn't know this was private property."

He says, "You're on the Sanctuary's land. You need to leave now."

I open my hands. "I can't. My car is stuck, and I've got a bum leg, so I can't walk out. I lost my phone and can't call for help."

"We saw you throw it over the cliff. That was a foolish thing to do."

I nod. "I totally agree with you. Now will you help me figure out a way to get out of here?"

Frogs croak in the silence that follows. Something rustles in the brush nearby, and I cringe. I want to get back to civilization and never set foot in a forest again. My father's dreams are not for me. I want people around and stores down the street. The dense wilderness is creeping me out, and so is the man standing before me.

Four people step out onto the rutted track that was marked on some map as a forest service road. They are wearing black clothes and carrying rifles. A short stocky one says, "He giving you trouble?"

The main guy who has me in his rifle sights says, "Not yet, but he's mouthy for someone stuck in the middle of nowhere."

A tall woman says, "Shall we shake him down, see what we can take?"

"Sure," the head guy says. "And search the car, but be quick about it. We need to shove him and his wreck over the edge of the cliff before someone tracks us down and finds him."

My heart races. "You can't do that."

"We sure can," the stocky man says. "This is our land, and we do whatever we want. Isn't that right?"

The others say, "That's right."

A jolt of pain zaps up my leg and I clench my hands, wincing.

"Something wrong with your leg?" the big man says.

"Someone shot me with an arrow. By any chance do you have a phone I can use?"

The tall woman says, "We do, but we're not sharing. We don't want traces of you to be tracked here. Come on," she says to the others. "Let's throw him and his car off the cliff. It'll take weeks or months to find him, if they ever do."

A high-pitched scream rings out, making my stomach curdle. I say, "What's that?"

She shrugs. "Just a bobcat."

"What would it take for you to change your minds and let me live tonight?"

41

BUZZ

I pace in my living room, and my dog lies on the floor with an eye open watching me. I pull out my phone and text Abby. 'How's Jack?'

She texts back seconds later. 'The same. He identified Craig as the one who hit him.'

My mouth falls open. But the knowledge that someone else is being blamed for my misdeeds doesn't make me feel better. In fact, it only makes the sinking feeling in my stomach worse. I text, 'Call me when you can. We need to talk.'

My phone rings a few minutes later. I say, "Craig did this to Jack?"

Abby says, "That's what it looks like, but I guess people can have false memories. It sounded like the police might send a guard to sit outside the room. If they do, I'll feel better with Jack being safe."

I run a hand through my hair. "What happened? Did Craig show up or something?"

"He did, and Jack pointed to him as the one who bashed in his head."

My gut churns with acid. I'll probably die an early death from stomach cancer or something terrible, from regrets and guilt eating at my organs. "What if Jack's wrong and someone else hurt him?"

She says, "I thought of that too. We might never know."

I blow out a breath. "It'd be awful if they accuse the wrong guy for something he didn't do. Craig would end up in prison for the scam against the elderly and serve a sentence for attempting to kill Jack."

"It's not up to us to decide if Jack is telling the truth. That's up to the authorities. Listen, I also called to say I can't find Johnson to talk about the money Jack owes. He's not picking up his phone, so I called the FBI woman, McNalley, and asked her to look into Johnson's boss, Mother Mercy. I want to convince her to give us an extension until next week, if I can. Maybe she'll take pity on us and move the deadline, you know?"

My mind whirs with a dozen different thoughts. I don't know about this Mercy person, and I don't care. I'm fixated on the notion that Jack fingered Craig as the one who caused his brain injury. The news is a relief, but at the same time, a worry, because at any time, the authorities could turn their attention to me, and I'll be the one landing in jail.

She says, "The FBI is looking into it, and we're still short the amount of money we need. I appreciate you offering to use your line of credit. I may still ask you to do that, if the deadline moves back."

"Okay, and tell Jack hi," I say. "I miss my best friend."

I flop on the couch. I'd give anything to have our lives go back to the way they were. It occurs to me that Irena must feel the same way, so I call her, but she doesn't pick up. She doesn't want to see me, and I don't blame her. She and Kelly are busy raising money, while I sit here alone, which is the story of my life, waiting for Irena to love me back.

42

MOTHER MERCY

Mother Mercy lay on his back on a stretcher in the hall. Doctors, nurses and aides swished past, wearing scrubs and serious looks on their faces. A young guy using a wheelchair said, "Help, someone help me. I got shot in the foot."

Mother Mercy squeezed his eyes shut and tried to block out the sounds of a busy hospital. Machines beeped. Voices called out. People wept. Sneakered feet strode by. He muttered to himself, tilting his head, and said in a high voice, "I brought you some food. Here this will kill you."

A male doctor in a white lab coat stopped and asked, "Everything okay here? We'll get to you as soon as we can."

The guy using the wheelchair moaned, and Mother Mercy said, "Thanks, I think that fella needs your help more than I do."

The doctor nodded and moved on. Mother Mercy observed his surroundings. What a hullabaloo was going on here. People crying in pain. Bloody heads and bandaged legs. This was not the quiet environment he preferred. Come to think of it, Elgin Johnson mentioned he'd been laid up at the hospital after someone shot him in the leg.

Mother Mercy frowned and grimaced as a spasm of nerve pain jolted him, from his phantom toe to the top of his head. He hoped whoever shot Johnson was in jail. He needed his right-hand man. He couldn't have him stuck in a hospital in the boonies.

His eyes narrowed. When he got back home, if Johnson hadn't called or texted, he was fired. Dependable workers were hard to come by, so Mother Mercy would do it himself and get the job done right. He'd drive his big boat of a car up to Mt. Vernon and Millersville and get his cash back, no matter how hard the dead-beat begged.

He smiled to himself. People called him a hard-ass, but he was only doing what was right and protecting his company. No leakage was his policy. Everyone paid him back in the end, even if it was with their life.

He fell asleep, despite the bedlam around him, and woke when a kind-eyed nurse patted his arm with a purple gloved hand. "Mr. Mercy? We're ready to examine you now."

He looked around. "What, out here in the hall without privacy?"

The nurse shrugged, and a doctor approached in a white coat. The nurse said, "All our exam rooms are full, but we didn't want to keep you waiting."

"Fine, then help me sit up. These old bones don't work the way they used to."

The doctor gently checked his arms and leg, asking if it hurt.

"Sure does," Mother Mercy said, wincing at the touch. "Right there."

"We'll send you for X-rays, but I suspect your leg is broken, and your arm is sprained. How carefully do you monitor your glucose level and control your diet?"

Mother Mercy scoffed. "I do my best, but we all slip from time to time, don't you think?" He forced out a nervous chuckle, because he didn't watch what he ate. Living like that was for sissies, worrying all the time. His mom passed away at sixty, so he knew life was short, and he was determined to enjoy each day he was alive, including inhaling a carton of fudge ice cream every night.

The doctor tapped a gloved hand on his clean-shaven chin. "Let's get bloodwork done too, while we're at it."

Mother Mercy waved a hand in the air. "I'm fine. It's just the broken leg and arm that are bothering me."

The nurse nodded. "We need to be cautious, just in case."

Mother Mercy said, "I don't really care about this other stuff. I've got to get back to work."

The doctor cocked his head. "I don't think you'll be doing that for a while. You might be laid up without a working leg, even using crutches, at first."

Mother Mercy clenched his teeth. "But I've got a business to attend to."

"You might want to take a few weeks off and have someone take over while you recover."

Mother Mercy said, "There is no one else."

The doctor nodded. "Try to find ways to give yourself time to recuperate."

The nurse smiled, showing a dimple in her cheek. "Someone will come by to take you for X-rays. It might be a while, given how many patients came in before you."

The nurse and doctor moved down the hall, and Mother Mercy bit his lower lip. He should never have opened the door to the neighbor. He wished he had his phone to check on Johnson's progress. If only he could drive to the hospital in Mt. Vernon and shake the cash out of Fishbone. But for that, he needed a driver and an errand boy. He'd have to think of who to call. Right now, he saw the downsides of living an isolated life. He hoped his only friend, The Cat, was okay in the house alone.

43

FRANKIE

Frankie drove south on I-5, passing Tacoma General Hospital, where the parking lot was mostly full. An aid car with flashing lights and a wailing siren drove by on the freeway, sending a chill up Frankie's spine. Sirens reminded her of the day her mother fell down the basement stairs and was taken to the hospital when Frankie was eight years old. She overhead at the memorial service, when lingering by a plate of sweet rolls, that her mother might have been pushed by her uncle when they were arguing.

Now, she drives and blows out a breath, shaking away the memory.

Brick glanced at her. "Ambulances creep you out?"

She turned off the highway, getting on an arterial. "Yeah, brings back old memories I'd rather forget."

"Know what you mean," he said. "Some things are best left in the past."

She parked in front of a house and said, "Sorry if this turns out to be a wild goose chase, but I had a hunch and wanted to follow up."

He covered a yawn with his hand. "Who needs sleep, anyway? It's over-rated."

They chuckled and climbed out of the car. The lights were on in the house, and in the driveway was a car registered to Mercy. They walked to the front door and knocked, but no one answered. Going around the house, she saw a pair of crutches on the lawn, and the back door was ajar. Pieces of a broken ceramic platter and bits of food lay on the back steps and paved walkway.

She said in a low voice, "Cover me, will you?"

He nodded.

She climbed the steps and rapped on the open back door. "FBI. We'd like to talk with you."

She stepped cautiously into the kitchen, where a cat was lapping up water. She said to Brick in a low voice, "Kitchen's clear."

Proceeding into the living room, she stood in the doorway watching two people go through papers on a desk. Birds chirped in a cage. Soft jazz played in the background. A woman in her thirties said to a man, "What's that?"

He shrugged. "Nothing much. Just documents about loans."

Frankie said, "Put your hands in the air. Which one of you is Mercy?"

Startled, the two held up their hands. "Not us, we live next door."

Brick said, "What are you doing here?"

The woman said, "Just helping out. Our neighbor's been injured and never leaves his house. I'm a Realtor and thought he might like to move into a retirement community, if he had enough money."

Frankie raised her eyebrows. "Sounds sketchy to me."

The woman said, "It's my line of work, so why shouldn't I help him move and enjoy the next stage in his life?"

"Did he ask you to look through his papers?"

The man said, "Well, no, but we thought we might be able to help the poor man. We'd better get going."

Frankie said in a stern tone of voice, "We'll need your names, phone numbers and address before you leave. We may have questions for you."

The couple provided the information, which Brick wrote down. He closed his pad and said, "Where is the homeowner? Did they invite you inside?"

The neighbor woman blushed and looked down. Her husband shrugged, pushing up the sleeves of a maroon cardigan worn over a yellow polo shirt. Clearing his throat, the man said, "We weren't really invited in. He sort of asked us to watch the place while he's gone."

Frankie said, "You said he. So, it's a man who lives here?"

"Yes, he lives by himself."

"Where did he go?"

The neighbor woman straightened to her full height of five-foot-two and said, "They took him to the hospital about an hour ago. He fell down the steps."

Frankie nodded, recalling seeing crutches in the yard. Something wasn't right here. These people were acting shifty, like they had a hidden agenda. Normal neighbors wouldn't be poking in your private financial information after you were taken to the hospital. She said, "Did the owner give you a key?"

He shook his head. "No, he didn't. But it all happened in such a hurry. Didn't it, babe?"

She nodded. "It all happened so fast. One minute he's in the kitchen, and the next they're taking him on a stretcher to the aid car." She snapped her fingers. "Just like that."

Frankie shot Brick a look, and they nodded to each other. Something smelled fishy, and it wasn't coming from the food and broken platter on the back steps. The cat meowed, rubbing against her leg, startling her. When she flinched, the cat jumped up on an armchair and stared into the cage at a pair of suddenly quiet birds.

Frankie eyed the two neighbors from next door. They might look innocent, but something in her gut told her they were up to trouble, examining private paperwork in the home. She said, "Do you know which hospital they took him to?"

He plucked lint from his maroon sweater and said, "Tacoma General, isn't that right, babe?"

She nodded. "I think so. I was kind of distracted, with everything going on. I nearly fell down the steps too, and food was flying everywhere. It was crazy."

Brick said, "I'll walk you to your house."

The woman shot him a nervous smile. "We're fine on our own."

"Yep, it's all good," said Mr. Sweater. "We'll show ourselves out."

Brick said, "We're looking for someone who goes by Mother Mercy. Do you know anyone by that name?"

They shook their heads.

Frankie crossed her arms. "Does the man who lives here have a female companion? Or does his mother live here?"

The Realtor opened her hands. "He's the only one we've seen here. But he gets his groceries delivered. No one else comes or goes."

Brick tilted his head. "Is there a basement to this home? Or an attic?"

The Realtor nodded. "The design is the same as our house, with a full basement and attic."

Frankie swallowed. This definitely called for a search warrant to go through every crevice of the house looking for a woman who went by Mother Mercy.

The couple went in the kitchen and stopped to whisper, heads close to each other, pointing at the gas range, before leaving. Frankie turned to her partner and said, "We need to find this guy at the hospital. Before we go, let's not touch anything but take a quick look around. They mentioned seeing papers about loans, so this guy, or his mother, could be Elgin Johnson's boss. We need a search warrant to enter the premises and log in evidence."

Brick said, "Not sure we have enough for a judge to grant a search warrant. Let's look around."

Frankie walked over to the desk, and the cat pounced, wrapping claws around her ankle. She yelped and jumped, wincing in pain. "The cat doesn't want us here, that's for sure."

On the desk was a stack of papers. The top one detailed a loan made to Jack Fishbone. A pink Post-it note was affixed to the page. In black felt tip marker, someone had scrawled, 'Johnson collecting by midnight tonight.'

Frankie said, "Looks like we found where Mother Mercy lives."

Brick took a quick photo of the document with his cell and said, "But it's not a crime to lend money or collect on a bad debt."

"True, it's the death threats against Fishbone that concern me."

He nodded. "There's a lot we don't know yet." He cupped his hands and called, "Hello? Anyone else here?"

He said, "Let's make sure no one is trapped inside before we leave."

Frankie grabbed a broom handle and poked the ceiling. "Hello?"

Silence greeted them. But then a scratching sound came from above. She saw the pull-down steps to the attic and said, "Do we check it out, or wait for a search warrant and come back later?"

They waited and listened. The only sound was the cat jumping on a worn recliner. Birds chirped. She said, "No one is calling out in distress. I think we wait and do it right."

He said, "I agree. Let's go."

They left by the back door, and she closed the door with gloved hands, so as not to leave fingerprints, to keep the cat inside. She said, "That cat was crazy, but I'd hate to see it get hurt."

Brick stopped, scanning the back yard. "No coyotes in these parts to grab it."

Frankie pointed at two sets of blinking yellow eyes on the fence and said, "But raccoons are in the area. They'd go after the cat for sure and make a snack out of it."

Brick knelt on the grass, pulled on gloves and took out a clear evidence bag. Rain drizzled down on his wool watch cap, and he pointed to a cell phone on the grass. "This phone might belong to Mother Mercy."

Frankie took out her phone and dialed. When her boss picked up, she said, "We found where Mother Mercy, the loan shark boss of the man threatening Fishbone, lives. We need a search warrant for his home. He had a fall and was taken to Tacoma General Hospital. We'll go interview him there."

Her boss said, "How soon do you need to get in the house to gather evidence?"

"As soon as possible," Frankie said. "We interrupted two neighbors in the unlocked home examining evidence. We'd like to get in and shut the operation down."

44

BUZZ

It is past dinner time and I should be inside watching a show or reading a book, like everyone else in my quiet neighborhood, but a force within driven by shame made me start a new project at night. I hammer in the back yard, ignoring drizzle coming down, and with each blow as I drive in a nail, I break the gentle hush.

My next-door neighbor calls to me from the fence. I shove my hammer in my tool belt and go over to Bert, who has lived next door for ten years. He pushes back his blue Mariner's ball cap and says, "It's a bit late for building, isn't it?"

I shove my hands in my pockets. "Sorry, did I wake Petosky? I hope not."

He smiles. "We just got him down, and it's been a

struggle. He's cranky and won't nap, and then he wakes up at night at the slightest sound, like the bedroom door creaking. We're exhausted."

I eye the dark bags under his eyes and wonder what it would be like to have children of my own. Abby and I split up before we had kids, and since then, I've been on my own for the most part. Irena is such a good mom. I'd like to have kids with her. But we would need to get back together before that could happen.

I say to my neighbor, "Sorry to disturb you. I'll quit for the night."

"What are you building, by the way?"

I cock my head, feeling awkward about the project. "It's a tiny building, just big enough for one person. Like a meditation hut, only better."

"I get it. A private get away all your own, where you can hide from life's troubles. I need that. Maybe when you're finished, you can build me one."

I say, "Say hi to Sherri for me."

"Will do." He waves and tromps up steps onto his deck, going in his house through a sliding glass door.

I gather my tools and store them in the shed, drying them with an old towel, so they won't rust from being exposed to rain. Heading inside, I stand at the kitchen sink and stare into the dark night, wondering how I can help Jack. I check my phone and see it is ten p.m. I'll go to the hospital and stand guard to protect Jack from the thug who is collecting money.

I open the back door and let Happy out in the yard to do his business. When he trots inside, I grab my car keys, toss him a treat and say, "I'll be back soon."

45

ABBY

Jack rests with his eyes closed, and I go online, continuing my efforts to locate Mother Mercy. The FBI agents may be working on finding her, but I can't sit on my hands. I want to negotiate with this Mercy person to move the deadline back a week to give us enough time to round up the money.

An idea hits me, and I reach for my phone and text Irena, suggesting she sell the violin to help make up the shortfall. She texts back: 'Busy selling shoes. I'll ask the violin maker again when I have time.'

I frown and reply: 'We don't have much time."

She texts: 'Can't talk now.'

My fingers tremble as I type: 'How money have we raised so far?'

I drum my fingers on my thigh, waiting, as seconds tick by, but she doesn't reply. Irena and Kelly are busy. I glance at my sleeping husband, and a wave of mixed emotions washes over me. I've loved him since I met him and now he's my husband, but finding him has brought threats, debts and sickness. My shoulders sink with the responsibility of caring for him, and I clench my teeth, reminding myself to get to work finding Mother Mercy. I must get the deadline moved.

My eyebrows arch when my search shows over six-hundred companies registered in the State of Washington with the word 'mother' or 'mercy' in the name. I review the first five pages but don't see any making loans, just charities and healthcare companies.

A headache throbs, and I rub my temples. My mouth is dry, so I get up and fill my cafeteria cup from the tap. Gulping tepid water, I shake my head. Our sweet beginning is turning sour. I was full of wonder when I found Jack, and we were married. Everything was glorious, and I was riding high on hope, love and joy. Now, I gaze in the mirror at a haggard forty-year-old woman with dark bags under her eyes.

I look at Jack and nod. I promised to give him my best no matter what, but dealing with his head injury is a huge challenge. I'm having trouble holding the vision that he'll walk out of here one day to lead a normal life.

A rap on the door startles me, and the cup of water falls to the floor. I grab paper towels and mop up the moisture as best I can. Straightening up, I see Buzz step in the room, and I break out in a broad smile.

I say in a low voice, so Jack won't wake up, "I'm so glad you're here. I've been down in the dumps."

He gives me a hug, and I lean into him, grateful for the support. He pulls away and says in a quiet voice, "It's a tough time, especially for you. I came by to stop Elgin Johnson from hurting Jack or you again."

I say, "I'm pretty sure he won't come back, but I appreciate you being here."

He says, "Do you think Elgin hit Jack and caused his head injury?"

"It's possible, but I'm not sure. Jack is convinced Craig did it."

He scratches his stubbled chin and whispers, "Why does he think Craig hit him?"

"He pointed at Craig but can't talk. They're going to put in a speaking device tomorrow."

Buzz frowns. "Seeing him like this is tough. He was so full of life and always kidding around." A flash of guilt flickers over his face, and he stares at the floor.

Something in his manner raises my suspicions, but I push aside thoughts that Buzz could possibly be responsible for Jack's injuries. Buzz has no motive. Besides, he's Jack's best friend.

Jack moans, putting a hand to his forehead. A machine connected to his breathing tube whirs, and monitors beep.

I pat his arm, saying, "Hey sweetie. Your friend Buzz is here."

Jack eyes Buzz and gives a slight nod. I say, "Rest, so you can recover. Tomorrow, they'll install a speaking device, so you can talk. Everything's going to work out fine." I smile, and he holds my hand. I say to him, "If I give you a pen and paper, will you write down why you think Craig hit you?"

He grimaces and squirms, shifting his shoulders.

I pull out a blank index card and pen from my bag and put them on his lap.

He blinks and shoves them aside. Paper flutters to the floor, and the pen drops, bouncing once on the hard surface. Buzz and I exchange a quick look, and I scoop up the pen and index card. "Maybe another time."

A nurse enters the room to take his vitals, and Buzz and I lean against the window sill watching. I glance out at what looks like a ten-foot drop to a roof below, lit up by street lights. If Johnson comes in and throws Jack out the window, my husband would die from the fall. I try to open the window, but the handle is fixed in place with screws and won't budge. I blow out a breath, and Buzz nods.

The nurse strides out of the room, the fabric of her scrubs swishing with each step. Buzz opens a narrow closet door and pulls out a folding chair. He sets it between the door and Jack. He says to me, "Take a nap, if you want. I'll stay awake all night."

I yawn, stretching my arms. "I could use a rest. Thanks."

I turn off the overhead light and climb in the recliner,

pushing it back, so the legs go up. I pull up a blanket and close my eyes, letting sleep overcome my worries, dreaming of happier times when Jack and I met on a beach for a secret picnic on a blanket spread on warm, soft sand.

My eyes flick open at the sound of men's voices. My heart pounds, and I leap up from the chair, ready to protect my husband.

Craig is frowning, with his hands on his hips, and saying to Buzz, "Jack screwed me over and sent me to jail. He doesn't deserve to have Abby fawning over him. He should suffer, like I did, so step aside."

Buzz clenches his fists and blocks Craig from moving toward the bed. Buzz says, "Leave this minute and don't come back. Isn't it obvious that Jack couldn't defend himself or event talk? His health predicament is precarious at best. Go on, get out of here and go home."

Craig plants his feet firmly on the floor. A vein throbs in his temple. "I'm not leaving until the score is settled. Move, or I'll hit you too."

Buzz says, "What kind of man are you who would hit someone who can't even raise his arms in bed?"

I step between the two angry men and say in a low voice, "Quiet down, both of you. Craig, I want you to leave. Buzz, I need you to stay because Elgin Johnson might be on his way, coming here any minute."

Craig glowers. "Who is Elgin Johnson?"

Buzz says, "A thug collecting money on a loan Jack didn't pay back."

Craig cocks his head. "Sounds like Jack, what a mooch. Why is the guy coming here?"

I put an index finger to my lips to remind them to keep the volume down. "Johnson gave us a deadline to pay it by midnight tonight, but he moved it up to eleven, and we don't have enough money."

I glance at Jack, whose eyes are closed. My hopes of him being well enough to go home is far off in the future. I shiver and rub my arms, wondering what this dark night might have in store.

Craig says, "Eleven is only an hour away. Jack was a leech who always had the last laugh. Not so funny, now, is it, buddy? Flat on your back, connected to machines."

I point to the door. "Leave right now, or I'm calling security."

Buzz says, "Get out of here and go home. He's in bad shape. Let him be."

Craig glares. "Jack deserves what's happening to him."

Jack's eyes open, and he grips the sheet. He points at Craig, jabbing the air.

I extend my arm and march Craig to the door. He shakes a fist and turns to walk out, but Elgin Johnson appears, wincing and limping, blocking the doorway with his big, broad-shouldered body. Johnson's face is scratched and smudged with dirt, and his knuckles are red and raw.

I gasp, and my hand flies up to my bruised sore neck, where he choked me. Buzz stands with his feet apart, raising his fists. Craig crosses his arms and leans against the wall.

I shake a fist at Johnson. "Stay away from Jack. We have an hour left to get the money, and I called the cops. They're on the way."

He half-smiles and says, "Sure, sweet thing, go on and tell more lies. The deadline is now. Where's the money, meatheads? Hand it over, or someone's going to get hurt."

46

IRENA

Kelly and I are working hard, sitting side by side at the kitchen table. I turn to her and say, "It's ten o'clock. You'd better go to bed, hon."

She pouts. "Not yet, not when people are asking questions and commenting on the crowdfunding page for Dad."

"Fine, but at eleven, you've got to shut it down and go to bed. Agreed?"

She nods. "Okay."

I let out a sigh. "We were short twenty-eight thousand dollars before. Where do we stand now?"

She tilts her head, like her father does when he is doing math. "With money you've raised from selling his sneakers, and donations, we still need eighteen-thousand dollars."

I rest my head on the table and groan. "We only have an hour left." I sit up and stretch my aching back. "I could try to sell the violin. That might be the only way we can come up with the money if we have enough time."

She says, "I was hoping you'd say that."

"You and Abby are on the same track." I pick up my phone and call the violin teacher. When he answers, I say, "I'm sorry to bother you this late, but I'd like to sell you the violin, so we can help Jack and pay back one of his debts."

He says, "Remember, I gave Jack that violin. I can't afford to buy back what I gave away in the first place."

I swallow and say, "We need to raise eighteen thousand dollars in the next hour."

Kelly wipes her eyes and gets up, going to the sink and looking out.

He says, "Short of doing something illegal, I can't think of how to help you. If only Jack had handled his money better."

I say, "It's a bit late for that."

The violin teacher says in a soft voice, "There is someone on an island near here who has money. It's possible I could arrange a private meeting for you to speak with her. But tonight is out of the question. She doesn't answer her phone after six o'clock."

"Please," I say, "text her or call her now? Jack's life could be at stake."

He says, "She won't like it, but I'll make an exception this once. I'll let you know if she responds."

"Can I have her number? And is her name Mother Mercy, by chance?"

He chuckles. "No, that's not her name. She goes by Tex, Tex Everett, and she lives on a private island. I can't and won't give out her digits."

I grip the phone tight. "Please tell her this is vitally important."

He says in a soothing voice, "I know. I've got to go. Wish me luck."

Kelly chimes in, and we say at the same time, "Good luck."

I hang up and say, "I've got to go to the bathroom. Be right back."

I go down the hall and close the door. In the privacy of the bathroom, I open the taps at the sink and lean over, crying and gulping for air. Jack, what did you do? Your memory is gone, and you don't even know what you did. You left a mess of things, and your friends and daughter are left trying to untangle the twisted knots you left behind.

I sit on the closed toilet seat and blow my nose, wiping my eyes. I won't breathe a word of it to Kelly, but our situation is hopeless. I splash cold water on my face, blot it with a towel, and take a deep breath, returning to the kitchen.

Kelly turns from the sink. "You okay?"

I open my hands. "Almost. Maybe in a week or two or in a few months, we'll laugh about this and take that beyond the bridge boat tour we talked about."

She groans. "You and Dad falling overboard started this. I've had enough of boating for a while."

Just then, my phone rings, and I answer it, assuming the violin teacher is calling with an update. Instead, someone with the Coast Guard says, "We have a report of a boat in distress near Thatcher Pass. Can you take the call? No boaters are in the vicinity, and the other rescue boat operators aren't available."

I frown, looking at the ceiling. "I'm sorry, but I'm not available. We have a family emergency going on."

"Are you sure? Our Coast Guard boat won't arrive in the area for an hour. The skipper said they're taking on water."

I glance at Kelly, who has her hands on her hips. I nod and consider the consequences. On this dark night, a boat may sink before the Coast Guard gets there.

I say, "Fine, I'll take the call. What's their position and contact information?"

I hang up and give my daughter a hug. "Sorry about this," I say. My pulse races, and I feel pulled to the marina. A boat may sink unless I get there and stop a disaster.

She says, "I know you have to go, but I wish you could stay home."

"Me too. Believe me, I'd rather be here."

I grab my gear and head to the door, resting my hand on the door knob. "Love you bunches and bunches."

"Back at you," she says, "and be safe."

"I'll be home as soon as I can."

I walk out and drive to the marina, wondering what awaits me on this rainy night.

47

———

MERCURY

I call my friend Tex, but she doesn't pick up. She lives on a private island near Thatcher Pass and flies to her waterfront estate on her plane or takes her boat from Millersville. We met at a mutual acquaintance's house in the islands and became friends. I've given her violin lessons, but she needed little coaching because she learned to play at age three, using the Suzuki method.

I leave a message for Tex to call me back, saying there's trouble in paradise and her help is needed. Then I text her for good measure with the same message. Making a cup of espresso, I sip a bitter brew and stare out at Cedar Channel. A blue-hulled ship goes by, but I barely pay attention. My stomach growls with hunger, but I can't eat. I'm too worried about what will happen to Jack.

My phone rings five minutes later. Tex says, "Tell me what's going on."

I explain the situation and how we're raising money to protect Jack from his past mistakes. She says, "You've spoken about Jack before and how he means well but trips over himself. I'll make it a loan."

I say, "He couldn't pay back a loan. He's lost his memory and can't eat or talk or get around. It'll be a while before he can work. Someone hit him and left him for dead."

She gasps. "Of course, I'll help. Is he the 'Missing Man' mentioned in the news?"

"That's him."

"I guess I could chip in and donate to the cause."

I chew on my lower lip. "How much can you give?"

She's quiet for a beat and says, "I'll give an even one-thousand. It wouldn't be right to give more to a stranger. I can't get a reputation for handing out money to just anyone."

"If you did, they'd be lining up at your door. Would you like to speak with his ex-wife or his daughter? Or his new wife?"

"He's been busy, hasn't he, despite having amnesia?"

I nod, thinking how Jack is the kind of guy women fall for, even though he is ill in a hospital, hooked up to machines. "We can't all be lucky in love."

I hear ice cubes clink in a glass, and she says, "No we can't. Tell his ex-wife to call me when she has time."

"I'll tell her to call you, and I'm sorry to bother you so

late. Go online to find the crowdfund raiser for Jack Fish-bone. Let me know if you can't find it."

We end the call, and I wipe my moist palms on my pants. Tex's gift is a huge help, but we don't have enough to make the threat disappear. I text the information to Irena, along with Tex's phone number, and lean against the cool wall in my one-person coffee shop. I sniff the air, inhaling the aroma of dark roasted coffee beans.

Living alone, I've been lonely since Jack left and now he doesn't know who I am. His friends are rallying around him, defending him against thugs and helping him recover his health. It is time for me to broaden my social circle.

I tug on my beard and think of the woman with sparkling blue eyes outside the hospital. She had spunk and was marching for Jack, despite the damp weather. I'll give her a call when this settles down.

48

FRANKIE

Frankie drove to Tacoma General Hospital with a firm grip on the wheel as she turned a tight corner. The tires squealed in protest. They were on the hunt and closing in on their prey. She said to her partner, "I'm pretty sure a judge will issue a search warrant, if what I saw in the house is correct. She could be laundering dirty money for cartels or mobsters."

Brick nodded and gazed out the window. He gripped the car seat, his fingers turning white. She slowed down. "Is my driving bothering you? Am I going too fast?"

He looked over and shook his head. "It's not your driving that's bothering me, it's the creepy house with the curtains closed and papers everywhere. I get the feeling something's wrong."

She shuddered. "Now that you mention it, the place

smelled off. But we can't let our imaginations run away from us."

She parked at the hospital, and they slammed the car doors, hurrying to the Emergency Room reception desk. They flashed their badges, and Frankie said, "We're looking for someone named Mercy. He was brought here by an aid car?"

The receptionist adjusted her black framed glasses and tapped on a keyboard. "We have one patient by the name of Mercy. You'll find him on a stretcher in the hallway. Hold on, I'll have someone take you back to that area."

A few minutes later, a nurse took them into the Emergency Room treatment area. She stopped at a man in his late fifties and said, "Mr. Mercy, these people from the FBI would like to talk with you."

His eyes grew wide. "What about? Do I need a lawyer?"

Frankie nodded to Brick, who said, "We have a few questions. Just routine inquiries. Do you know a Jack Fishbone?"

Mercy picked at his blue bathrobe.

Frankie said, "We've been in your home, so don't lie to us. The door was open, and the neighbors were in there."

His face flushed, and he clenched his jaw.

Brick said, "We believe you made a loan to Mr. Fishbone, and you've been trying to collect on that overdue debt. Is that correct?"

Mercy looked away and stared at the mint-colored green wall.

She cleared her throat and said, "Does Elgin Johnson work for you?"

Mercy shrugged and didn't meet their eyes.

Brick said, "Is there anything you'd like to tell us?"

Mercy asked, "What about my cat? Was it around?"

Frankie and Brick exchanged a quick glance. Brick said, "The cat was inside. We closed the door, but it isn't locked. We're getting a search warrant to go in and search the premises, and we can make sure the cat's okay."

Mercy said in a loud voice, "Help. I need a doctor or a nurse."

A woman in her thirties wearing scrubs hurried over. "How can I help you?"

He said, "I need to go home right now."

She frowned and put her hands on her hips. "You haven't had your X-rays, and your leg and arm may be broken. We can't discharge you."

He swung his leg over the side of the stretcher and grimaced. "No matter what you say, I'm getting out of here. I never should've come here."

She said, "If you leave, it'll be against medical advice and insurance won't cover your visit."

"Look, I don't care. Get me some crutches, or do I have to scream to get them? I'm asking nicely, but I'll do whatever it takes."

She held up an index finger. "Wait right here. I'll tell the doctor and get you crutches. Don't move."

Frankie murmured to her partner, "Looks like we shouldn't have mentioned the search warrant." Her phone rang, and she stepped away to answer it. Abby said, "We need you here now. The man who choked me is back. Elgin Johnson is in Jack's room."

Frankie said, "We sent an officer to guard the room, but they might've been delayed. I'm in Tacoma, and it'd take too long for us to get there. Call hospital security. I'll work on it from my end."

She hung up and said to Brick in a low voice, "Wish we could be in two places at once. Johnson is confronting Fishbone in his hospital room. I'll call the boss."

Brick nodded, and she said, "Keep an eye on Mercy. I'd like to detain him, if we have enough to make the charges stick."

She dialed her boss, who answered on the first ring. Frankie said, "We're with Mercy at the hospital, and it looks like he's going to do a runner. I think we can get him on wire fraud, money laundering and possible witness tampering. I saw what looked like wire transfer records in his home. Mercy's employee Johnson is threatening Fishbone right now in his hospital room in Mt. Vernon. I just got a call from Fishbone's wife sounding terrified."

Her boss said, "I sent a guard to make sure Johnson couldn't get to our witness. Wonder what the hell happened? I'll get right on it."

Frankie said, "I think we have enough to detain Mercy, and he's a flight risk."

"Absolutely. Hold him. Don't let him leave."

49

———

JACK

There is a commotion by the door, with people milling around. Buzz, who Abby says is my best friend, has his back to me and his fists raised, as if he's protecting me.

I close my eyes. I can't do anything about the group crowding by the door, and if I die, that's what will be. From what I've heard, I've done enough damage, and it might be just as well if I quietly pass away in this bed tonight.

I squeeze my eyes shut and listen to the whirring of a nearby machine. Except for my wonderful wife, I don't have much to live for, and I'm a burden, hooked up to machines and saddled with debt. Sure, she'd mourn me, but she wouldn't have to worry about my health. If I die in my sleep tonight, it will be a fine time to exit the planet.

50

IRENA

My pulse races as I climb in my boat and check the oil. I want to finish this job and head home as fast as I can. While the engine warms up, I call the skipper of the boat in distress and take his credit card payment. I release the lines and leave the marina as rain pelts the windshield and wiper blades swish back and forth. With fifteen knot winds and a one-foot chop, conditions are excellent for making a night run.

Beyond the breakwater, I push on the throttle and floor it, flying through the waves. I switch on the search light and watch for floating logs. If I hit a deadhead bobbing below the surface, the damage might put a hole in my hull, and I'd be the one making a distress call.

I turn the wheel to enter Cedar Channel, and the current carries me west. The twenty-eight-car ferry to

Cedar Island is stopped for the night, and all is quiet as I move past Millersville. The channel opens into Rosario Strait, where a tugboat is pulling a tanker, heading south. I head west for Thatcher Pass, and my thoughts drift to Jack's overdue debt. I glance at a brass wall clock by the barometer. Our deadline is in forty minutes, we still need eighteen-thousand-dollars.

Sweat pricks my armpits, and I flick off the cabin heat. I approach the area and scan the bay where the boat in distress should be, but don't see the powerboat. Checking the coordinates, I putter through the bay a second time, aiming the search light.

Grabbing the marine radio microphone, I hail the powerboat but get no reply. I repeat the call and wait a few minutes before letting the Coast Guard know the vessel in distress is not in the area.

Broadening my search to scour nearby bays, I cuss under my breath. Aiming the spotlight, I search other bays near Blakely Island. Finally, I spot a forty-two-foot powerboat bobbing at anchor in a quiet cove. The lights are off inside, and I circle the boat to check the hull, which looks solid and sound, without a gash in the side. The bilge pump isn't running, and the vessel is riding above the waterline, making me doubt the boat is taking on water.

I pull alongside and rap on the hull. "Permission to come aboard?"

Waves slosh against the boat, and clouds move overhead. I breathe in briny air and pound on the cabin door. A man inside says, "Coming."

A man in his thirties slides opens the cabin door. His glasses are askew, and he yawns. "Yeah?"

I clear my throat. "I'm Irena Fishbone from Nimbus Boat Rescue. Permission to come aboard?" He stares at me and doesn't slide the door open, so I say, "Your boat was taking on water?"

He shakes his head, and the smell of alcohol wafts my way. "We're all set. We panicked when a ferry went by. All those big waves, you know?"

I say, "Would you like me to take a look before I go? There's a minimum charge for a call out at this time of night."

He waves a hand. "We're fine. Sorry to bother you."

My hands clench and I say, "Have you notified the Coast Guard to not come? Making a false distress call could land you in big trouble."

I stride to my helm. I pull away from the once-panicked boaters who are now probably fast asleep, and I call the Coast Guard with an update.

Checking my phone, I read a text from the violin teacher, and my eyebrows shoot up when I see he gave a phone number for Tex, who lives on an island near Thatcher Pass. Taking a chance, I text her to say I'm in the area, if it's not too late for me to drop by. I put the engine in idle and drum on the steering wheel, waiting to see if she'll respond. I hope she might donate even more money if she meets me. Shaking my head, I marvel at how Jack's problems have led me to beg for money.

Waves splash against the side of the boat. I bite a fingernail and hope Tex will respond. It's a desperate play to ask for additional help from a stranger. According to what Mercury Thunder texted, Tex chipped in a thousand bucks, which is fabulous, but that means we still need to raise seventeen thousand dollars. My mind swims with conflicting desires to get home to Kelly, or speak with a stranger and beg for cash. I frown, frustrated at how I was called out on a dark, rainy night for no reason.

I call Kelly to check in, and she says, "Nothing came in from the crowdfunding since you left, except a big donation from someone named Tex, so that helps."

"It does, but it isn't enough. I'm going to try a weird idea. I'm near Tex's house on Grand Island and hope she'll want to see me tonight. If she texts me back soon, I'll meet her. If not, I'll come right home."

"What happened with the boat that needed help?"

I snort. "Waves from the ferry scared them, and they called for help but picked up anchor and moved without letting me know. I found them in another bay. Have you heard from Abby? I wonder what's going on at the hospital."

"Nothing from her. Everything has been quiet since you left."

My phone dings with a text. I glance at it and say to

Kelly, "Hon, Tex, who gave money to help your dad, wants to see me."

Kelly says in a tight voice, "Now? Isn't it late to do that? Come home instead."

"I wish, but this could help your father in a big way. If I meet her, she might donate more money."

Kelly sighs. "Fine, but call me when you're heading home. And be careful."

"I will, baby girl. I won't stay long."

She says in a tight voice, "Eleven o'clock is in twenty-five minutes."

My heart thuds, and I glance at the barometer, which is dropping. The brass clock ticks ahead, thwarting our efforts to save Jack. What a fool he was to get mixed up with thugs and what I suspect may be a money-lending mobster for the sake of sneakers.

I say, "I've got to give this a try. Love you, got to go."

I hang up and reply to Tex's message: 'Be there in a few minutes.'

51

IRENA

A steady breeze pulls strands of hair from my ponytail, whipping them in my face, as I tie up at a private dock on Grand Island. I check my dock lines to be sure the boat is secure and glance up a paved road toward Tex's house, the first one on the right. I can't stay long, and I'll be fighting the current on the way back to Millersville.

I stride up the hill, breathing hard and chastising myself. I should be home with Kelly, not running a fool's errand. The likelihood of this visit resulting in a fix for Jack's dilemma is minimal at best. I should just turn around, jump in my boat and race home instead of chasing a thin thread of an idea woven with misguided hopes.

I approach a large timbered home with tall windows and vaulted ceilings. Lights inside create a warm glow, glimmering on a pond in front. A pang of envy shoots through me because it would be peaceful to live here, looking out at the water and watching storms roll through. But it might be boring at times, and we'd be far from friends and a grocery store. I'd have to home school Kelly or take her by boat to a one-room schoolhouse on a nearby island.

My phone dings with a text, bringing me back to the present. Buzz sent it an hour ago, but it just came through. He wrote: 'Your dad followed me to my house and asked where you live, but I didn't tell him. Hang in there. Hope to see you soon.'

I bite my lower lip and continue to the front door. I blocked out thoughts about my father coming to town for years. I could try to hide from him, which is unlikely to work, or gather the courage to confront him head on.

I lift a heavy ring hanging from a metal lion's head and knock on the huge wood front door. A woman in her sixties with shoulder-length blond hair opens the door and flashes a white-toothed smile. "Welcome," she says, gesturing for me to come in. "Irena, isn't it?"

I step inside and let my shoulders relax in the warmth. Chamber music plays in the background. A fire flickers to my left. Wood floors with area rugs make the space look elegant and appealing.

She points to a couch. "Let's sit over there. May I take your coat?"

I shake my head. "No thanks, I can't stay long. I have a

teenager to get home to, and the weather is turning. I appreciate your inviting me at the last minute and I won't take much of your time."

We sit on the couch, and I shrug off my coat. I feel more secure with my jacket by my side, as if I might need to run out at a moment's notice. I say, "I wanted to thank you for donating to Jack's cause."

She studies my face. "But that wasn't enough, was it? You need more money by midnight? Or was it eleven p.m.?"

I nod. "Our group of friends is trying to deal with it, but the debt collector threatened to hurt Jack if we don't pay what's due by eleven. It's been very stressful for all of us."

"Oh, dear, that's horrible. Could I get you a glass of wine or coffee or tea?"

"Thanks, but I'm running solo and need a clear head while I'm underway, with no time for bathroom breaks. Maybe another time? It must be wonderful to live here, with all this surrounding you." I give her a tentative smile.

She says, "Living here is an amazing gift. But sometimes I get lonely, if I'm honest. Books and music can only do so much. We had a power outage last week, and I spent two days reading in the dark by flashlight and talking to myself. So, it's a pleasure to meet you, and I admire what you do. You must be a resourceful person to run a company on your own."

I sigh, soaking in the praise. "Thanks, it's challenging at times."

She meets my gaze. "Would you like to have a silent partner? I'd be interested in helping you in your business."

I cross my arms. "I'm not sure. I've never considered something like that."

She says, "Would you be open to it perhaps?"

I nod slowly, but a tiny hesitation knocks at my brain. I clear my throat and sweep aside my reservations. "Maybe. Mercury Thunder knows you, so I should be able to trust you. And I do have a haul out scheduled for bottom paint, which isn't cheap. But the idea of not having complete control over the company scares me. And what about the legal paperwork? I don't have the money to do that."

She eyes a silver tabby cat, curled up in a ball on a braided rug by the fire, and smiles. "I have a lot of money sitting around, and it's not making me happier than the next person. I'd like to give you thirty-thousand-dollars on a hand shake, and I'll transfer the money as soon as you leave. We can write a few lines on paper and sign it. I think this partnership could be beneficial to both of us."

I stand and release a whoosh of breath. "With that much money, I could pay off Jack's debt and have enough to help with the boat haul out. Are you sure you want to do this?"

She rises and says, "Yes, and I think I'd enjoy getting to know you and your friends in the future." She frowns.

"Except for that Craig fellow who was jailed on charges of white-collar crimes. I don't think he's someone I'd want to know."

I hold out my hand. "Agreed, and it's a deal. Let's shake on it. I hope you don't expect a big return on your investment."

She laughs and waves a hand in the air. "That's the benefit of being rich. I can invest in what makes me happy but doesn't pay large financial rewards. But I would like monthly status updates, and we can get together to go over your business plan."

I say, "Thank you so much. Let's sign, and I'll go home to my daughter and tell my friends the good news."

She cocks her head. "Are you sure you want to give part of the money away to help a friend? You might need it for repairs or a new engine. Think hard before you give it away."

We walk to a wooden farm table with chunky legs. She takes a pad of paper and writes, 'I am investing in Nimbus Boat Rescue as a silent partner. I do not expect large returns on my money, but I would like regular progress reports and stories.' She writes the date and her name, adding her signature.

She hands me the pen, and I write, 'I accept the investment of thirty-thousand dollars from this silent partner and will use it wisely and provide progress reports." I sign the document and write the date and my full name. I take out my phone and photograph the documents.

She smiles. "Would you prefer a check or for me to wire money to your account?"

I tap a finger on my chin. "Would you write two checks, one for seventeen-thousand that I'll sign over to the debt collector, and a second one for the rest to Nimbus Boat Rescue? And thank you so much. You don't know how much I appreciate this."

While she writes the checks, I pull out my phone to text Abby and tell her we have the money, but my phone doesn't have cell service. She hands me the checks, which I zip into my down vest pocket for safekeeping, and we exchange a quick hug.

She goes to the door and opens it. "Go on, I know you're in a hurry. And if you ever want to come stay the night with your daughter, I'd love to meet her, if she's anything like you. And some day, I may want to be more involved in running your business. I have a lot of experience, and that's how I was able to afford this. We can run it through a limited liability corporation and pay dividends."

Her gaze meets mine, and I realize she plans to be more involved than I was led to believe. I pull on my rain coat and give a quick wave. "Thanks so much. I'll be in touch."

As I run to my boat, rain hits my face, and I break out in a wide smile. While the engine warms up, I dial Abby, but the call doesn't go through. I text her, but see, 'Service unavailable.'

I mutter, "There's a price to living in paradise."

I untie my dock lines, stow them onboard and turn the boat toward home. Compared to this remote outpost, my small town is a bustling commercial zone. I steer and chew on the inside of my cheek, thinking of my dad and hoping he won't decide to settle in Millersville. He must be out on parole, but I don't want to talk to him to find out, not after the way he treated my mother when I was young.

I cross Rosario Strait, where rum runners plied the waters during Prohibition in boats without lights at night, and when I enter Cedar Channel, I call Abby.

She picks up and says in a nervous voice, "I can't talk. Something's going on."

I say, "But I have the rest of the money."

She hangs up, and the line goes dead. I tap my fingers on the wheel and glance at my speed. I'm going ten knots against an opposing current, so I increase the speed, and the engine whines, working hard.

A flash of lightning strikes to the east in the foothills, and distant thunder rumbles. I furrow my brow and turn south toward the marina. Inside the breakwater, the halyards clang against masts. I dock my boat, hop out and secure the dock lines. Running through the wind and rain to my car, I sniff the sea air. Wind whistles and moans, making eerie sounds. A storm is coming.

As I drive home, an irritating thought taps at the back of my mind. Should I get to know him for Kelly's sake and give her a grandfather? I shake my head and turn into our driveway. He was a horrible father, and he doesn't deserve the privilege of being a grandfather. I don't trust him, and as far as I'm concerned, Kelly won't get near him.

I climb out of the car and glance at the curb, where a gray sedan is parked in front of our house. When I open the front door, I'm greeted by a man's hearty laughter. A man in his sixties is sitting on the couch with Kelly. I slam the door shut, drop my bag on the floor and face the father I haven't seen in over thirty years.

52

ABBY

My heart pounds as I step into the hall and find a nurse. I point to Jack's room. "A man is threatening my husband. Please, call security."

I dial the FBI agent and when she answers, I say, "Elgin Johnson is in Jack's room, threatening to hurt him."

She says, "The guard we sent must have been delayed."

I frown. "We need them here now."

"I'll check on my end. We can't get there. We're in Tacoma. I've got to go." She hangs up.

Entering Jack's room, my mouth falls open. Beads of sweat dot Buzz's upper lip and he has Elgin in a headlock. Elgin's face is red. He grimaces and stomps on Buzz's foot, and Buzz flinches, weakening his hold.

Elgin whips around, striking Buzz on the side of his head. He says, "Who else wants to take me on?"

Craig rolls his eyes and crosses his arms, standing between Elgin and Jack. "There must be a better way to make money. You should go into a different line of work."

Buzz and I exchange a quick look. Maybe Jack will make it through this confrontation after all.

Elgin leans against the wall, panting. "This is my last job, then I'm out. I'm going to buy a few acres near town. I want to get one of those miniature donkeys."

Craig opens his hands. "You can't have just one donkey. You have to have two, so they don't feel alone."

Elgin rubs his neck, which I hope hurts as much as mine, where he choked me.

Craig says, "There's a lot you don't know. We're friends, and we stand up for each other." He belts Elgin in the mouth, and Elgin's head snaps back. Jack makes a noise. I go over to Jack, and he points a trembling hand.

Craig kicks Elgin's bad leg, and he falls to the floor, moaning.

A security guard rushes in the room, and she says, "What's going on here? Is this man bothering you?"

Buzz, Craig and I say at the same time, "Yes."

The guard says, "I'll take him away."

Buzz says, "Don't trust him. He'll escape if you even blink an eye."

The guard straightens up to her full six feet, grabs

Elgin's arm, and he limps toward the door. A sturdily-built woman in a dark suit blocks the doorway. She flashes her badge, whips his hands behind his back and snaps on hand cuffs. "FBI. Come with me, and don't give me trouble. You're wanted on a number of charges."

He says, "I didn't do anything."

She cocks her head. "You're going down for wire fraud and tax evasion, and I'm just getting started."

Jack points at Elgin, and I say, "Is Elgin the one who hit you?"

Jack nods. I say to the FBI agent, "Better charge that man with witness tampering, while you're at it."

Buzz turns pale. His jaw clenches, and he stares at the floor. I go over to Buzz and say, "Is everything okay? You look like you saw a ghost."

We watch the agent haul Elgin away, and Buzz goes over to Jack. "I'm sorry, buddy, for what you're going through. I really am."

Craig says, "Cut the pity party. Jack doesn't deserve sympathy after what he did to me."

Jack's face turns red, and his heart monitor and blood pressure alarms erupt, issuing high-pitched beeps.

I turn to Craig and point to the door. "You're upsetting him. Leave and don't come back."

He scowls. "Jack got what was coming to him. He lied to the police. And Abby, I underestimated you."

I usher him out and watch as he lumbers down the

hall, disappearing around a corner. I swallow and think I'll take a boring life, please, with one serving of a husband and two bowls of ice cream. I cross my fingers and tell myself in a month's time, he should be feeling better. We just have to tough it out until then.

A nurse comes in the room, silencing the monitor alarms. She turns to us and says with a concerned look, "His condition is serious, and he needs to rest. No more visitors."

I turn to Buzz and give him a quick hug. "I'll let you know when he's moved out of intensive care." Buzz nods but won't meet my eyes. He gently closes the door, and the fact that Buzz had Jack's wallet niggles at the back of my brain. The authorities checked the wharf where Jack was found. Shouldn't they have found his wallet?

I call the FBI agent, but she doesn't pick up, so I leave a message and mention Buzz found the wallet. I hang up, and Jack gives me a slight nod. I send Irena a text, saying Jack is resting and can't have visitors until tomorrow, if then. She doesn't answer, so I figure she's busy. I send a second text to tell her Elgin Johnson was carted away by the FBI.

I wait for her to reply and stretch my arms, yawning. When I don't hear from her, I turn off my phone for the night. My back aches, my eyes are dry, and I can't wait to fall asleep. I kiss Jack on his whiskered cheek and say, "Sleep well, my love."

I flick off the overhead light and slump into the recliner, pulling the leg support up and pushing the back down. Spreading a blanket over my body, I snuggle into a comfortable cocoon. My eyes fly open minutes later when someone knocks on the door and rolls in a cart. A young woman with short hair says, "I need to do a blood draw."

53

IRENA

I glare at the man making himself comfortable on my couch sitting by my daughter. My father has his arm thrown over the back of the sofa, and he's laughing at a joke. The jackass who choked my mother and pushed her to the kitchen floor won't get sympathy or an open invitation from me, not in my home, not anytime, not now.

Kelly smiles. "Hey, Mom, Granddad is here. Now we finally have more family around. Isn't it great? We're having a great time. He has so many stories to tell."

I give the mean-tempered man a steely gaze. My mother and I were glad to be rid of him when he was sent to prison many years ago. We laughed and sang driving west on I-90 and north on I-5 until we turned off and ended up to this out of the way waterfront town.

When my mom rented our first apartment, we stepped

inside and she gave me a hug, saying, "Don't mind the musty smell. We're make it the home we never had. Your father will never find us here in Millersville. I made sure of that."

I unfurl my fists and force myself to sit down in an armchair facing him. I'd like to smack him in the mouth for hurting my mom. He tossed pancakes in the trash that she made for me before school. The memories make my jaw tense. I'd like to take him down from his haughty high perch.

He cocks his head. "Everything okay there, cookie?"

I'm as still as a statue. "My name is Irena."

He smiles. "Renie, Renie, your mother picked that name for you. I wanted to call you Heather, but I was outvoted."

Kelly looks from him to me, her mouth falling open. She grabs a throw pillow and hugs it tight. I nod to her and say to him, "I didn't invite you in my home."

He stands and opens his arms. "Don't be that way, sweetheart. Let's start over. Come here, and I'll give you a hug."

I slowly shake my head. "I'm not doing this, Dad. Mom made sure that you wouldn't find us. You have no right to barge in like this. Did they let you out on parole?"

He beams. "Yep, I didn't deserve to be locked up all that time. It was only a bar brawl." His face shows a long scar from his left eyebrow to his chin, perhaps from a fight in prison.

I arch an eyebrow. "A man died at your hands."

Kelly's eyes open wide, and she stares at him, inching away.

"Look, I know it's been a long time, but I'd like to make amends. I'm in this program where I'm asking for forgiveness for my wrong doings."

I stand, crossing my arms. "You should be begging forgiveness from Mom, but it's too late for that. My best parent passed away. I won't forgive you for what you did to her, so keep driving to another town far away from us."

His eyes narrow, and his mouth forms a thin line. His hands clench, and he stands, holding my gaze. "You're not in charge of me. I'm finished with that life, being locked in a cell and told what to do. We're going to be a happy family, and you don't have a say in the matter. Chickadee here will go fishing with me and for picnics whenever I want. I'm her grandfather, and I'll dictate what happens, on my terms with my timing. End of story."

I step over and grab the fireplace poker as a weapon, opening the door and gesturing outside. My phone dings with a text, but I ignore it. "You're mistaken, and that's not how it's going to work. I want you to leave and don't come back, or I'll call the cops. How will your parole officer feel about your coming here to harass us?"

A muscle twitches in his jaw, like it used to before he lashed out and hit my mom. A vein throbs in his forehead, and I used it as a weather forecast when I was young, warning of mood swings and fists lashing out. When the vein thumped in his forehead, I'd run outside. But if he blocked the doorway, I'd run and hide in the bathroom, locking the door. I whimpered and hid as guilt washed over me because I'd left my mother to take the brunt of his anger.

Now, I take a deep breath and stand tall. I'm not a child cowering before a mean-spirited man. I'm a grown woman who is protecting my child, like my mother did.

He sneers. "You wouldn't call the cops on your dad."

I snort. "I will. Now leave and don't come back."

He stomps to the door and stops to stare at Kelly, making my stomach churn with acid. He glowers under dark brows and jabs at finger at me. "I have rights as a grandfather, and you can't stop me from seeing Kelly."

Shaking my head, I say, "You won't see her again, because I won't let you."

He grins. "I'll be back as often as I like. You can't stop me from seeing Kelly."

Kelly stands. "It's my decision, and I'll make up my mind."

I say, "Over my dead body."

He glares at me. "Kelly and I will get along fine without you, Renie."

I step in front of her. "I forbid you to see her or come here."

He puts on his cowboy hat and steps outside. "It doesn't matter. I'll be back."

I slam the door in his face, and my hands shake as I lock it.

Kelly says, "Do you have something to tell me?"

"Let's sit down."

We sit on the couch side by side, and my knees tremble. I say, "Your grandfather has a temper and lashes out. You're not safe with him."

"But he seems so nice."

I nod. "It's part of his act to get close to someone, like he did before he married my mom. After they got married, everything changed. I won't go into specifics, but you need to stay away from him. He'll lure you in at first and then you're in his web of power, trapped but wanting to run."

Kelly lets out a sigh. "I wanted to have a grandfather. I was happy to meet him."

"I know it sounds confusing. Some people have two sides, and they only expose the nice one until they wrap their tentacles around you and have you in their control. Then they show their real self."

She tilts her head. "I'll stay away from him, if he comes here or goes to school."

"I'll talk to the school and explain the situation."

She says, "Don't tell my teacher. That would be embarrassing."

I pat her knee. "I'll protect you, but you must stay away from him. If we have to, Tex on Grand Island invited us to stay overnight. We could have a little getaway there."

A smile spreads across her face. "Can we bring Dad when he gets better? And Abby, of course."

"Sure, she said our friends are welcome, and she'd like to get to know us. We could all go over and hang out for a day when your dad's better."

She blows out a breath and rests her elbows on her knees. "I wonder when he'll recognize me. His memory loss can't last forever, can it?"

"The doctors don't know if it'll come back, so we have to be patient. In the meantime, young lady, I'm going to wrap my arms around you and hug you like a Giant Pacific octopus." I hold her and squeeze her, and she laughs, squirming out of my arms.

She says, "What else happened with Tex? Did she give you more money?"

I unzip my down vest pocket and pull out two checks, waving them in the air. "She paid me to become a silent partner in Nimbus Boat Rescue."

We stand and dance around the room until I stop and say, "I need to let Abby know. My calls didn't go through to her from Thatcher Pass, so I'll call her now."

I pull out my phone and dial Abby, but I get a notification that says she has turned off notifications. Checking my messages, Kelly and I listen to one from Abby. I hang up and say, "That's good news. Elgin Johnson was hauled away by the FBI."

We throw our hands in the air, hooting and hollering, and dance in the living room. Breathing hard, I wonder how Buzz is faring but push the thought away. I'm home with my daughter celebrating that the debt collecting thug has been banished. I'm through with Buzz.

Kelly says, "What about the money we raised?"

"We'll use it to pay his other debts."

She says, "But he owes you child support."

I nod. "That will be the last debt paid. It doesn't seem right to ask people for donations and take some right off for myself."

She frowns. "I wish he remembered me."

I pat her shoulder. "He loves you very much."

"But he doesn't know who I am."

"We'll bring photos next time to show him. Maybe that'll spark his memory."

She blinks back tears, and her shoulders slump. "I guess."

54

FRANKIE

Frankie and her partner turned Mercy over to other agents to hold him until questioning. A judge granted a search warrant, and they drove to Mercy's house, located on a quiet street in North Tacoma. Before entering, they pulled on crime scene booties and gloves. When the first floor was clear, Frankie said, "Let's check the basement." He said, "Then the attic."

She opened the basement door, and the hinges creaked. She flicked on the light and went down the wood steps, weapon at the ready. The windows were covered with pieces of plywood.

Brick followed her and aimed a flashlight at a chest freezer. He walked over to it. "Care to guess what's inside?"

"Frozen carcasses of dead beats who didn't pay him back."

"That or frozen dinners. Kitchen doesn't look like it's

used much. Here we go." He threw open the lid, and they peered in through a misty cloud.

"Doesn't that beat all," Brick said, taking a few photos.

She said, "Each one is labeled nice and neat. Look, this one is Lucy." With gloved hands, she shoved aside plastic packages. "This is Gloria."

"Here's Harriet. Each one has a name and date. Must be cats who passed away."

She picked through the contents, and a sliver of light caught her eye, coming from under a door. She gestured to him, and he nodded.

"FBI," he called. "Open up."

The door remained closed, so he kicked the door in. She followed him into the room, and they crossed their arms, surveying two rows of green leafy plants, ten in all, under grow lights. Frankie sniffed the air. "Doesn't look or smell like marijuana."

Brick pointed. "He's got an irrigation system set up."

He touched a leaf, rubbing it between his fingers. She did the same and sniffed her hand. "Catnip," she said. "Takes all kinds."

They tromped up the stairs, and he said, "Just the attic left to clear. I want to examine the evidence. I bet we have this guy ten ways to Sunday."

She nodded. "I agree."

He pulled down the attic steps, and they gingerly climbed up and stood in the attic, inhaling dust. Cobwebs brushed across her eyes, and she pushed them out of her face. She aimed her torch around the room.

Rain pattered against the window in the attic. A mouse ran across the floor. She wrinkled her nose at an unpleasant odor. She said, "You smell that?"

"Yep." He aimed his flashlight into a dark corner. "Bingo. There it is."

Frankie joined him and took in the crime scene. "This will send him to prison."

She studied a desiccated body shrouded in cobwebs, sitting on a rocking chair. A red-checked apron tied around the waist was covered with a layer of dust. A strand of pearls hung from what may have been an older woman's neck, with a tag labelled in black felt tip marker that read: 'Mother Mercy.'

Frankie shook her head. "Such a shame."

He nodded. "Might be his mother, or someone else. We'll find out."

They hustled down the dusty attic steps and placed calls. Other agents joined them, and they pored over evidence in the home, bagging items. The medical examiner arrived and, hours later, the body was taken away. A yellow crime scene tape was put up outside.

They were about to leave when Brick said, "The cat, we forgot about the cat."

Frankie glanced next door, where the Realtor and her husband were stepping out of their house bundled in heavy coats and hats, carrying umbrellas. She said, "They might be willing to take the cat."

The Realtor waved and smiled. "What's going on? We saw a van and stretcher. What happened?"

Brick said, "You'll read about it in the papers when there is news to share. In the meantime, would you take care of Mr. Mercy's cat? I'm sure he'd appreciate it."

The neighbor looked at her husband, who was scowling, and said, "It would be a good business decision. Maybe he'll sell to us at a low price." He nodded, and she said, "Sure, we'll take the cat."

Frankie and Brick cornered the cat and lured it into the cat carrier with shrimp and salmon that had fallen onto the grass. At the last minute, the cat bolted, but Brick scooped it up and gently lowered it into the container. He snapped the lid shut and handed it to the nosy neighbors. "Here you are. I'm sure he'll appreciate it."

Driving away, Frankie let out a slow breath. "Let's formulate a plan for Fishbone. I want to see if we can trigger his memory of who hit him and about the scam."

Brick said, "His friend Craig had strong motives to hurt him."

"Let's transport Fishbone tomorrow to the scene where the EMT's found him and see if that jogs his memory."

He checked his watch and yawned. "Be nice to get a full night's sleep, but that's not happening. It's already past four in the morning."

"Killers and white-collar criminals never stop, so we don't get to rest."

55

JACK

A nurse checks my vitals early in the morning, before the sun comes up, and a parade of doctors stops by. The verdict is they'll keep me in the hospital for another few days to monitor my condition. Abby is strangely quiet, pacing the room when we're alone. Later, a nurse comes in to install a speaking device, and Abby holds my hand.

The nurse says, "How're you feeling?"

I say, "My head hurts, but the pain isn't as bad as yesterday. But I've been worrying about something. What if they lose my missing piece of skull?"

She adjusts her yellow-framed glasses. "They keep careful records. I wouldn't worry about that."

Abby nods.

I focus on speaking and say, "But it could get mixed up with someone else's."

The nurse pats the bedside rail. "It'll be fine."

Someone knocks on the door, and a man in a blue jacket rolls in a wheelchair. A woman in a blue windbreaker follows him. Abby whispers, "They're FBI agents." She gets up and greets them and introduces me to them, but I know who they are. My problem is recalling what happened before I landed in the hospital, not who I saw yesterday.

The nurse checks my vital signs.

Special Agent McNalley says, "We're taking you to Martin Wharf, where you were found. We hope that might jog your memory."

Abby says, "He's not well enough to travel."

Special Agent Brick says, "We spoke to his doctors, and we have permission to transport him by ambulance to the wharf."

Abby bites her lower lip. "I don't want him leaving the hospital."

McNalley says, "The doctor cleared him for this trip. The sooner we get started, the faster he'll be back in his hospital bed."

Brick says, "EMT's will watch over him in the ambulance."

Abby trembles, staring out the window.

McNalley says, "Aren't you curious to see if his memory will come back?"

Abby slowly nods.

Brick says, "This trip might jog his memory."

I say, "I'll go. I want to find out who did this to me."

The nurse says, "I'll get you ready."

Abby says to McNalley, "Did your team scour the scene where Jack was found?"

McNalley says, "Yes, we did a thorough search."

Abby pulls a wallet from her purse and holds it out. "Our friend Buzz found Jack's wallet at the wharf. He said he found it on the road when he went back to see where he dropped off Jack that night."

The agents raise their eyebrows, and Brick pulls out a plastic evidence bag, opening it. "We'll take it and check for fingerprints."

Abby drops the wallet in the bag and says, "My fingerprints are on it, and Buzz touched it. I wonder if Craig hit him and touched the wallet?"

McNalley says, "We'll see."

Brick goes out to the hall and returns with two men in dark blue shirts and pants and black shoes. Brick says, "The EMT's will transport you to Martin Wharf."

McNalley says, "They're trained technicians and have a mobile intensive care unit in the ambulance. You'll be in good hands."

Abby gazes at me with her arms crossed. "I'll go with you and ride in the ambulance."

An EMT shakes his head. "I'm sorry, but we can only transport the patient."

Abby sighs. "I'll drive myself then. I want to be there in case you remember something or have an emergency. I don't want to lose you again." She laces her fingers through mine.

I squeeze her hand and say, "I'll be fine."

An EMT rolls the wheelchair over to me and sets the brake. I hang my legs over the edge of the bed, and he helps me get in the wheelchair while Abby watches. She pulls out a warm jacket and helps me put it on. The nurse wraps blankets around me, leaving the bright yellow non-skid hospital socks on.

Abby says, "I'll bring an umbrella." I look out at a blue sky, and she shrugs. "In case it rains."

McNalley steps over and says to Abby, "On second thought, it might be best if you stayed behind in the room."

Brick nods. "That's right. We're making a quick trip, just over and back, with no distractions."

Abby stamps a foot. "I'm coming, and I won't get in the way. Just try to stop me from staying close to my husband."

Brick and McNalley glance at each other. McNalley says, "Fine, you're welcome to come along but stay in the background while we handle this."

"Okay," she says, looking at the floor, but something in her manner makes me doubt she is capable of staying on the side lines and watching the action take place. I give her a smile, my beautiful wife with the heart-shaped face who found me when I was a lost John Doe.

They roll me in a wheelchair down the hall, with a

cart carrying a breathing support unit. Going down, the elevator hums, and the agents stand straight with their hands in front. An EMT stands to my right. Abby glances at me and fiddles with her purse strap.

We exit the elevator. Rolling outside, fresh air blows past, and my shoulders relax. I look around, feeling grateful to be alive and out of the hospital.

They roll the wheelchair up a ramp into the ambulance and strap me in place. Abby waves, sending me an air kiss, and says, "See you there."

The ambulance bumps ahead and then the ride smooths out. I face a side wall, and a technician is seated, surrounded by an array of medical equipment. I glance outside and wonder what we will discover at the wharf, if anything. Smiling to myself, I believe my taking this trip means there's hope for my recovery.

56

JACK

As the ambulance rumbles along, I drum my fingers on the arms of the wheelchair. The air is chilly, and my feet grow cold. What if I disappoint the agents and come up dry, dredging my ailing memory banks? The possibility of my recalling who hit me seems far-fetched. The ambulance turns, bumps down a dirt road and pulls to a stop.

The back of the ambulance opens, and they roll me in the wheelchair down a ramp. I study my surroundings. A wooden building sits at the end of the road. To my right is an old dock overlooking blue water. It feels somewhat familiar but laced with evil vibes, and my hands fist. My pulse picks up. I'm in no shape to run, but this place feels dangerous.

Abby parks her car and runs over, but Agent McNalley puts out a hand, stopping her from coming to me.

McNalley says, "Let's let him soak it in and see if he can step back in time."

A powerboat races across the water, the engine whining. Birds chirp, and a squirrel scampers by. The dirt road is damp from recent rain. A sensation of having been here before creeps up my spine. Hairs on the back of my neck stand on end, and I am sure I was here before.

Brick says, "You were here at night, is that right?"

I say, "Yes, I think so."

He says, "How did you get here?"

Looking over the water, I say, "I think it was by boat."

A car pulls up, screeching to a stop. Buzz opens his door and runs over, but Brick puts out a hand and says, "Stop right there. Don't interfere."

Abby stands by Buzz, and they cross their arms, looking at me. I cover my face with my hands and say, "I don't like it when people stare at me."

Brick goes over, talking to them in a low voice, and Abby and Buzz step away and look at the water. Before Buzz turns away, he grimaces and gives me a last look.

Something about the stricken look at Buzz's face brings back a tendril of a memory, like a feather floating through air. I try to grab the thought before it disappears. Waves shush quietly against the wharf. I smell creosote on the wharf pilings and briny salt air.

Suddenly, I'm thrust back to a dark night when Buzz dropped me off here. I wince and remember him yelling and running toward me, like he did from his car to join us just now. The look on his face that night was one of pure hatred. He lashed out, his fist struck my face, and I fell back. The memory fades, and that's all I recall.

I touch my head and moan. I'd rather blame Craig or Elgin for my brain trauma, not my best friend. I try to summon other, different memories to pin the wicked act on anyone but Buzz.

"You okay?" Abby asks. She moves toward me, but Brick puts a finger to his lips, shakes his head and motions for her to step back.

I hold up an index finger and squeeze my eyes shut to reconnect to what happened. In my mind, I create a scene where Craig belts my face, but it doesn't resonate. I try to picture Elgin slamming his fist into me, but I can't see it. In the end, I'm sure Craig and Elgin are not the culprits.

I open my eyes as a plane flies overhead. A humming-bird flutters in the air nearby, and I stare at the broad shoulders of my supposed best friend.

I say, "Why did you do it?"

They all turn to me, and I look at Buzz. He frowns, running a hand through his hair. His right eye ticks, and his face flushes, turning red.

I grip the wheelchair arms. "Why?"

He clears his throat. "Your memories are messed up, and you're mixing me up with Craig or Elgin. Maybe they did it together. Irena told me she saw them talking on the street before Craig went to jail."

The FBI agents nod to each other and move toward

him. Buzz opens his hands and says in tight voice, "I didn't do anything. He's mistaken, and we can't believe what he says. When I dropped him off here, he was fine. He must've hit his head after I left."

I say, "You brought me here by boat as a favor. But you got angry when I mentioned taking Abby, Irena and Kelly with me. You lost it and slammed your fist into my eye, and I fell back and hit my head."

He shoves his hands in his pockets. "I bet Elgin Johnson crept out of the bushes and hit you, and Craig might've helped him! Elgin was really angry you didn't pay him back."

I say, "That didn't happen, and you know it. They weren't here that night."

Abby looks from Buzz to me. She comes over to me as the agents walk toward Buzz. He yells, "You know it was Craig. You guys haven't gotten along for a long time. I heard you two arguing about the scam when I stopped by. He has a temper. He hit you that night!"

I say, "No, you did it. You left me on this dirt road. You didn't call for help."

Buzz runs for his car, but McNalley tackles him and cuffs his hands behind his back. The agents walk him to their car. As they push his head down to get in the back seat, he yells, "Abby, take care of my dog. Happy likes you." McNalley closes the door.

Abby races to my side and kisses my cheek.

Brick trots over and says, "We're taking Buzz in for

questioning. Jack, did you remember anything about the scam?"

"No, not yet."

Brick says to the EMTs, "You can take him back to the hospital now."

57

MOTHER MERCY

The FBI agents put Mother Mercy in a windowless interrogation room, read him his rights and left him alone for what felt like hours. His handcuffed wrists ached, his arm hurt and his leg throbbed with pain. He never should have let that pushy, pesky next-door neighbor into his kitchen. She started all this trouble.

He worried about his cat and chewed on the inside of his mouth, but then his thoughts wandered to Elgin Johnson. He wondered if Johnson had collected the money or dealt with Fishbone in a more permanent way. If he got out of this mess, Mother Mercy wanted to throttle Johnson and dump his body off a boat, feeding him to crabs. No one would go looking for him. He had no family or friends to report him missing.

An agent with slicked back black hair came in the room and slid a photograph to Mercy's side of the table. "Tell us about the woman we found in your attic."

Mercy shrugged. His arm ached from falling down the back stairs earlier at home. He didn't recall the event clearly, but he thought the neighbor, Jennifer or Jessica, had tripped him. A doctor at Tacoma General said his arm wasn't broken, just sprained. But his leg was another matter.

With FBI agents by his side at the hospital, he had been whisked through X-rays, and the leg was soon set in a cast. A nurse gave him crutches and slipped a sling over his arm.

The male FBI agent tapped a manicured fingernail on the photo of Mercy's dead mother. He'd never confess to the crime, but he had been fed up one day and locked her in the attic when she was up there looking for an old family photo. She'd been harping on him, criticizing his work and saying he should be dating, but at the time he was a one-legged guy in his forties living with his mother. No one in their right mind was going to want that. He hadn't tested his theory, because he was busy ignoring the pounding on the ceiling and the smell, when the noise finally stopped upstairs. But that was years ago, and what mattered now was that he helped people who couldn't borrow money elsewhere. He rescued the downtrodden, and no one would dissuade him from that fact.

The agent tapped the photo. "Is this your mother?"

He cleared his throat. "I want an attorney. I'm not saying another word."

58

ELGIN

The jail cell door closes and locks with a snick. I wrinkle my nose at the smell of sausage farts and strong body odor. A big brute of a man steps away from the wall. "What are you in for?"

I sit on the lower bunk to rest my aching right leg where they removed the arrow, and the man stands next to me, crossing his arms, looking down. "Move," he says, "or I'll mess you up. That's my bunk. You should've asked first."

I jump up and rub my throbbing leg. Glancing at the upper bunk, I have no idea how I'll climb up there. I lean against the wall and frown. This mess is Fishbone's fault. Until I met him, I avoided spending time behind bars. If only he'd paid on time.

My beefy block of a cell mate slides into bed, leaning

back and putting up his feet. He says, "What're you in for?"

I shrug. "I didn't do anything."

"That's what everybody says. What's the charge?"

"Some stupid white-collar crime."

He arches an eyebrow. "Fancy pants, are you?"

I shake my head. "They have the wrong guy. I don't know what they're talking about."

"What do you do for money?"

I run an index finger over my lip, thinking fast. "I raise miniature donkeys."

He slaps his knee and chuckles. "I'd like to get one of those when I get out."

I cock my head. "You can't have just one. You need two, for company."

He grunts. "I didn't know that. My last cell mate ran a scam, but they sprung him before he could tell me about it. You must know how to make a fast buck, being accused of white-collar crimes."

I say, "Sorry to disappoint you, but I'm just a guy who cares about animals."

59

IRENA

Abby texts me that Jack has a speaking device, and they took him to Martin Wharf to jog his memory. 'He remembered Buzz was the one who hit him.'

My jaw falls open. I text, 'You sure? They're best friends.'

'The FBI took him in for interrogation.'

My fingers tremble as I reply. 'Do you think he did it?'

'I'm not sure, but that's what Jack says. Come visit when you can.'

'K, will be good to see you.'

I lean against the kitchen sink and stare into the backyard, where recent rain and wind have blown blossoms off the magnolia tree, scattering petals on the ground. Buzz has been my rock through much of my life. I drum my fingers on the cold porcelain sink and nod, because deep in my heart, part of me believes Buzz did it.

Everything changed the day we went out on Craig's boat, and the rogue wave swept Jack and I overboard into a weird time of turmoil. I take a deep breath, feeling as if a storm blew through town, leaving still silence in its wake. I'm adjusting to Abby being Jack's wife. We'll pick up, minus a few friends, because life moves on. Circumstances shaped Craig and Buzz into worse versions of themselves. We witnessed their true natures, exposed by crises Jack caused. I sigh and rub my aching temples, because all this chaos was brought on by his sneaker fetish. It's a waste of time and money that could've been spent on my daughter.

Kelly comes home from school and drops her backpack by the front door.

I give her a hug. "Shall we go visit your dad at the hospital?"

She smiles. "I was hoping we'd go today."

"Let's bring photos to see if they jog his memory."

We pick three photos, so as not to overwhelm him at first. One was taken ten years ago, when Kelly was three. Jack is holding her hand, and they are smiling into the camera. Another shows Jack with his arm around Kelly's shoulder after a dance recital last year. The third is a group shot, showing our gang on Craig's boat.

Looking at Buzz, Kelly, Jack, Abby, Craig and me, I say, "How things have changed since then."

She nods. "They have."

She slaps together a peanut butter sandwich for a snack, and we hop in the car. I drive to the hospital in Mt. Vernon, and traffic is slow on Highway 20, but the mood in the car is optimistic. Kelly eats her sandwich, and I sniff the air, smelling peanut butter. It is a beautiful afternoon with blue skies as we go by farm fields with deep furrows. Blueberry bushes are putting on a show, standing out in striking flaming crimson red.

I say, "This is crazy, but Abby says the FBI took your dad to Martin Wharf, and he remembered who caused his brain injury. Buzz did it."

Kelly stops eating and turns to stare at me. "Buzz wouldn't do that. They're best friends."

I shrug. "I know. It's hard to believe. I guess the FBI and police will sort it out."

"But what about Happy, Buzz's dog? Where will he go?"

"Let's find out when we see Abby."

I park, and we rush into the hospital at a record pace, Kelly's long legs matching mine stride for stride. When we walk into Jack's room, Abby comes over and hugs us.

She says, "I'm so happy you're here. What a day we've had." She glances at Jack and says, "Go ahead and tell her."

Using a speaking device, he says, "I'm tired. You tell them. Hi, Kelly and Irena."

Kelly grins. "Hi, Dad."

We gather around Jack's bed, and Abby tells us what happened at the wharf and how Buzz ran to his car but was tackled by FBI agents, who took him away.

I say, "It's almost hard to believe."

Jack says, "Not when you're alone on a dock with him. I told him I wanted to take you three with me when I left town, but Buzz hit me and I fell back, hitting my head. Then I blacked out."

I say, "You remembered that? Is your memory all the way back?"

He says, "Just part of it. I know Abby says I was married to you, and Kelly is my daughter. Kelly, will you hold my hand?"

Kelly stands at his side, putting her hand in his, and tears stream down her cheeks. I leave them to their private moment and motion to Abby to step out in the hall. I whisper to her, "It's amazing he remembered Buzz hit him. I never knew Buzz had such a temper. Did you?"

She tilts her head. "Maybe it was a moment of temporary insanity and he lost control. If he hadn't done that, Jack wouldn't be fighting for his life."

"It's odd Jack's memory only came back about that and nothing else."

She folds her arms. "It struck me as odd, but maybe memories come back in flashes, stimulated by triggers, like sights, smells and sounds."

"Makes sense. What about his dog? Who is taking Happy while Buzz is in jail?"

"He asked me to take the dog, but I can't while Jack's here. Can you take him?"

I smile. "We'd love to. Before we go back in, I want to say I love you, and I'm sorry you're going through this. You deserved a fairytale wedding and honeymoon, but instead you're here."

She beams. "There's nowhere I'd rather be than by his side, helping him."

I give her a hug and say, "You're good for him. Let's go see how they're doing."

We walk in the room, and Kelly is showing her father the photos we brought. He says, "There's my beautiful Abby, and my wonderful, talented daughter."

My throat closes tight with tears because this is exactly what Kelly needs and wants. Our world is resetting to spin on a better-than-before axis. A tear trickles down my cheek at the wonder of witnessing this moment between them.

During a pause in conversation, I say, "Kels, Abby says we can take care of Happy until they get out of the hospital."

She grins. "Let's go get him now."

Jack says, "Take care of him."

Kelly kisses his cheek, and I wave goodbye as we go out the door. A half hour later, we pull up to Buzz's house. Happy barks inside as I jiggle my key in the front door. A man waves from a gray sedan parked across the street, and a flood of worry sweeps over me, but I go back to my business of rescuing the dog and taking him home.

We clip the leash to Happy, and his tail swishes in the air. Kelly takes him outside, and I grab dog food and his bowls. I stand at the door and lock it, letting out a heavy sigh. What a shame it came to this.

Three black sedans skid to a stop out front, and FBI agents leap out of the cars. McNalley says, "Stop right there."

I drop the sack of dog food and set the bowls down on the front porch. "Don't hurt us. We just came to take the dog."

McNalley strides over. "That's okay. But we can't have you removing any evidence or entering the premises again."

Five minutes later, we're on our way, heading for home with Happy. Kelly sits in the back seat with the dog, petting him. She says to the dog, "Everything will be okay. My dad is getting better. Don't worry, we'll take care of you until Abby and Dad leave the hospital."

I blink back tears and park at our place. Pinned to the front door is a note that says 'Call me as soon as you can. Dad' There's a phone number on it, but I take the note, rip it to shreds, letting pieces flutter to the lawn. I refuse to reopen that part of my past.

60

BUZZ

The FBI agents put me in a small room and read me my rights. My hands are sweaty, and I wipe them on my jeans. I grimace as it hits me that I almost killed my best friend. Any punishment the authorities dole out will be less than the self-recrimination harping in my head.

McNalley says, "Tell us what happened that night on the wharf."

I shake my head. "I want a lawyer."

McNalley and Brick exchange a quick look. Brick taps the table and says, "This is your chance to tell us the truth. We'll go easier on you if you talk to us."

"I want a lawyer."

They leave the room and a few hours later, a woman opens the door to the stuffy room. She is wearing a white shirt and a dark pantsuit, with dark hair pulled back in a bun. She sets down her briefcase and says, "I'm Wanda Bates, your lawyer, and they have no evidence, just accusations from someone with a traumatic brain injury. He could be making it up or blaming it on the wrong person. I'm going to get you out of here on bail."

I clench my jaw, recalling how I lost my temper and walloped Jack that night, so hard he fell back on his head. For that, I will never forgive myself. "Thank you," I say.

She leaves, and I sit alone in the room berating myself. Hours later, I walk out, but the clock is ticking on my time as a free man. Eventually, they'll find a way to pin Jack's near death on me. My heart hammers at how I ruined my life. I almost killed my best friend and lost my one true love. I arrange for an Uber to get a ride to my car at the wharf, but when we arrive, a tow truck is hauling it away.

I jump out in front of the tow truck and wave my hands. "That's my car."

The driver says, "This car is part of an investigation. You'll have to wait until it's over. Sorry about that."

He drives away in a cloud of dust, and I climb back in the Uber. The driver is a woman in her thirties chomping on gum as if her life depended on it. Her clothes give off a faint odor of musty mildew. I say, "Drop me off at Jackson Bridge, will you?"

She studies me in the rear-view mirror. "You're not planning to jump, are you? Because there's a hotline we can call if you're having a hard time."

I wave the idea away and force out a chuckle. "I want

to stand there looking out remembering a boat trip with friends when life was easy."

She nods and drives, snapping her gum. "Makes sense. Who are these friends?"

My face heats with shame. "A group of close friends from high school."

61

IRENA

Kelly and I are getting ready for bed that night when there is a knock at the door. My pulse picks up, and I hope my father isn't back to bother us. I pull back the living room curtain and see two police officers on the front steps. I wince because whatever news they're bringing can't be good.

I tighten the tie on my green terry cloth bathrobe and open the door. "Yes?"

A man in his late forties with short salt and pepper hair says, "Irena Fishbone?"

I swallow hard. "Yes, that's me."

A blond female officer in her thirties says, "May we come in? We have something to tell you. It would be best if you're sitting down."

I take a shallow breath. "Of course, take a seat."

Kelly comes in the room wearing a purple sweat shirt

and sweatpants. She stops in her tracks and says, "What's going on?"

I say, "They came to tell us something."

The officers sit ramrod straight in chairs, and Kelly and I perch on the sofa, holding hands. Whatever is coming can't be good news from the serious looks on their faces. Happy scratches at the back door and barks. I had let him out before bed to do his business in the fenced back yard and was about to let him back in when the officers arrived.

Kelly hops up. "I'll get him. Don't say anything until I come back."

Happy bounds in the room, getting pets from the officers and me. Kelly sits on the floor with her arms around the dog. The air in the room is thick with tension.

The female officer clears her throat. "We're sorry to tell you but witnesses say Bud Wiser jumped off Jackson Bridge. He listed you as his emergency contact, so that's why we're here."

I wipe tears from my eyes. "Are they sure it was him?"

The male officer says, "His wallet, shoes and car keys were found on the bridge."

Kelly sniffles and buries her head in the dog's fur.

The blond officer says, "His body hasn't been recovered. There's no telling where his body might be, due to currents in the area. Search and rescue were called, but they didn't find him."

I groan and rest my head in my hands. Buzz certainly

had burdens to carry, and I'm sure I was part of them. I gaze at the officers and ask, "Is there a chance he might have survived the fall?"

He says, "It's been known to happen, but the odds make it unlikely."

I break down crying, and Kelly pats my knee. The dog pushes his nose in my face, licking me. I look up and say to the officers, "We almost got married. I can't believe this. They say he jumped?"

He says, "Two drivers saw him but couldn't stop in time. It was over in a flash."

Poor Buzz, to be driven to do that, to take the final exit. I shake my head and wipe my face, patting the dog's head. The dog whines, as if sensing the news about his favorite human, and Kelly says, "We'll take care of you."

As the officers stand, the man says, "We'll need you to come collect his things at the station when you have time."

They walk out the door, taking with them the best part of my past, my youthful joy and laughter, my carefree teenage years, my friend and protector who became my boyfriend until we went out on Craig's boat that disastrous day. I close the door softly and lock it.

Someone knocks at the door, and I see my neighbor, so I open it a crack. She says, "Everything okay? I saw the police were here."

I figure I might as well tell her the news because it will get around town anyway with the speed of lightning, and she taught Buzz in grade school. "I'm sorry to say this, but Buzz jumped off Jackson Bridge today."

She claps a hand to her mouth. "Oh, no. I scolded him the last time I saw him."

The black and white patrol car drives away, and I lean against the door jamb. "We need time to absorb the news. I'll talk to you later."

I close the door and lock it, leaning back with tears streaming down my cheeks. What if I'd been kinder to Buzz instead of judging him? I could have been a better friend. He must have been upset that his best friend was hurt. Even if he was responsible for hitting Jack and causing the head injury, I wouldn't want him to be dead.

Kelly comes over and hugs me. The dog nuzzles us. I say, "What a shame. I loved him. He was a sensitive soul, and he'll take his secrets to his grave."

62

IRENA

The next day I head to the police station, wiping tears from my face as I drive. Alone in the car, I talk to myself. "Why, Buzz, why? It's not right."

I pull over to the curb in a quiet part of town, leaning against the steering wheel and crying. I didn't want Kelly to hear me weeping, so I waited to be alone to surrender to how my heart is broken. A chill runs through me as I picture his final leap.

I blow my nose, take a deep breath and drive, parking by the police station. At the front counter, I say to a middle-aged woman with bangs, "I'm here to pick up Bud Wiser's things. The officers said I should come in."

"Just a minute." She gets up and disappears in back. Fifteen minutes later, I sign a paper. My eyes are blurry with tears, and I'm light headed. It doesn't seem real.

I walk out the door with items in a clear plastic bag

and lean against the brick wall. A part of me thinks this is a cruel cosmic joke. But if he hurt Jack and almost killed him, I can see how the guilt would drive him to make a rash decision.

I hurry to my car and drive, turning toward Buzz's house and letting myself in. Prowling around for clues to his final thoughts, I come to the second bedroom and turn the closet door knob, but it is locked. I try the keys on his key ring, but they don't work.

I clap a hand to my mouth and snap out of my fog. I've got to tell his employees at the bookstore, and I need to talk to Abby and Jack. They'll need to process the loss too.

63

JACKLYN

Armando, the framing foreman, points to the site for Stone Estates and tugs on his toolbelt. "I can do the job, but your son was late making payments. Can I count on you to pay on time?"

I cross my arms and look out over town to Cedar Channel, where I almost lost my life one night. "I'll pay you on time. I have funding from backers, and I'm waiting for permits to put in infrastructure and begin building."

My dog barks, chasing a flock of birds, and his ears flap as he runs. I bring my dog to meetings, because if I left him in the yard, I fear my son would take Buddy to spite me and break my heart.

Armando taps his lips. "I probably shouldn't mention this, but I heard your son is telling people in the city planning department not to approve your permit."

I grimace. I won't let Dusty get in the way of Stone

Estates becoming a reality. I'll sweet talk the city planners, and I know the head of the planning department's mother, and I'll tell her how this project will benefit our town.

I say, "Thank you for telling me. My husband, who passed away, would want me to go ahead with the project. He came up with the concept."

He says, "You said you have backers?"

I nod. "A group of business owners are backing the project, and I applied for a commercial loan."

"Hope it goes through. The cost of lumber is going up, so the sooner you can lock in the loan, the better. Also, just so you know, a few subs were tight with your son, so they might try to rip you off by padding invoices."

I cock my head. "Can you give me names, so I know who to watch out for?"

He shrugs. "I can't tell you that. It would kill my business. But double-check your invoices. I look forward to working with you."

I say, "I'll keep you updated about the financing."

He gestures to town and beyond that, to Cedar Island in the distance. I shudder, recalling how my son and daughter tricked me into taking a short vacation by saying, "Go for a few days. You'll feel better and come back a new person." They were right, because I came home with a steel plate for a spine, a hard heart toward my son and gratitude for being alive.

He points to the San Juan Islands. "It'll be spectacular, living up here."

I say, "Maybe you should buy one of the homes and live here."

He shakes his head. "I build them but don't buy them. Maybe one day."

"I look forward to working with you. If by chance my son tries to bribe you to slow progress on the job site, please let me know. I'll make it worth your while to share that."

He gazes at me. "I heard he moved out of town, and he's renting a cabin near the mountains. Pretty damp and cold over there, with not much to do."

"I wouldn't know. I cut ties with him after I got home from Shore Lodge." My phone rings, and I see Irena is calling. I say to Armando, "Thanks for meeting me. I'll be in touch. I've got to take this call."

He waves a hand and walks to his mud-splattered truck.

I answer the phone and say to Irena, "How're you holding up? I heard the awful news about Buzz."

64

IRENA

Five weeks later, on a crisp, sunny day, a group of us board my boat and we putter out of the marina, heading for Tex's place. We're wearing life jackets and the mood is subdued as I navigate Cedar Channel. My guess is our minds are drifting to the one person who will never join our group again. My throat closes with tears.

I sit at the helm and steer across a relatively calm Rosario Strait. Turning into Thatcher Pass, I hug the shoreline and keep an eye on the depth finder and chart to avoid submerged rocks. A ferry boat comes up behind, blasting the horn, and Abby squeals.

I say to her, "Made you jump, didn't it?"

She laughs. "Sure did."

I say in a low voice, "I feel bad about Buzz."

Abby rubs my back. "Me too."

Jack sits strapped in where Kelly usually sits. He says, "He must've had a dark side we didn't know about. I sure saw it that night at the wharf."

I say, "If they find him and by some miracle he's alive, will they charge him with a crime?"

Jack says, "They have enough on him to send him to jail for many years."

I say, "Even if he didn't mean to do it?"

"Even so," Abby says. She pats Jack's arm and says, "We're lucky Jack is alive. That was a close call."

Kelly pats her dad's back. "Does your skull feel strange where they put it back together?"

Jack makes a scary face, making his hands like claws. "The operation was a complete success, my dear. They made me into a monster who nibbles at thirteen-year-old girls who like to dance. Mahahah."

He tickles her, and she laughs. I let out a sigh, relieved to hear laughter. I held a service for Buzz last week at Seafarer's Memorial Park, and everyone in town came. Not an eye was dry in the crowd.

I slow the boat's speed and head for Tex's dock at Grand Island. The sound of laughter comes from the stern, where Jacklyn and Mercury, the violin teacher, are talking. The two dogs, Buddy and Happy, are wearing life jackets. Their noses twitch as they sniff the sea air, probably laden with the scent of seals, otters and Orca whales. I grin at the dogs and glance toward land, looking forward to feasting outside with the blue water before us.

Kelly and I tie the lines to dock cleats and help others climb off the boat. We make sure everything is ship shape on board and the panel instruments are turned off before following the others. Jacklyn and Mercury lean toward each other as they walk, deep in a discussion about classical music. Jack is using a cane and helped by Abby, who is holding his arm, making their way slowly up the hill.

Kelly says to me, "Do you think we'll play croquet or badminton?"

"We'll see what Tex has in mind."

Hairs on the back of my neck stand on end, and I turn to see if someone is watching us. Out in the bay is a boat that looks very much like Craig's. I frown, because this is not a day for chasing shadows, it is a time to be joyful and celebrate Jack's recovery. I must be imagining things.

I wrap my arm around my daughter's shoulders. "Come on, let's see what she has planned. We could just hang out and watch boats go by."

Kelly cocks her head. "You're getting better at lazing around."

I nod. "I'm working on it. That's my goal."

She says, "I like how we watched a movie together last night."

I gaze at the blue sky and smile at her. "You know I love spending time with you."

She says in a quiet voice, "Do you think Dad really lost his memory? Sometimes I wonder if he was faking it all along."

I glance at Jack. "He'd never do that."

But in the back of my mind, doubts caw in my ear like a relentless crow, and I shake my head to clear my thoughts before greeting our hostess for the day. I give Tex a hug and say, "This is my daughter, Kelly."

She beams at Kelly. "I hear you're a dancer, and I want to hear all about it. I have games planned for this afternoon, and I'll need your help."

Kelly says, "What kind of games?"

Tex gestures to the front lawn. "A scavenger hunt, table tennis, badminton and, if people are up for it, volleyball."

Kelly points to wooden balls and a row of mallets. "What about croquet?"

Tex grins. "Yes, but I'll warn you, I play a mean game of croquet. I know it's bad form, but watch out, I may win on my home turf."

Soon, we're laughing and seated outdoors at a long table under the shade of a maple tree. Fairy lights twinkle overhead in tree branches. We fill red, yellow, purple and green tall plastic tumblers with lemon water or iced tea. Beer and wine are served, but I stick with ice tea to stay sharp as the skipper on our trip home.

My mouth waters as I serve a helping of pasta with sun-dried tomatoes, feta cheese, black olives and chopped fresh basil. Forks clatter as we dig in. Down the table, Kelly sits with her father. She tells a story and waves her hands in the air. Jack nods, grinning at her, and my heart warms to see him back from the brink of death, listening to every word our precious daughter utters.

Across the table, Abby talks to Jacklyn and Mercury about Jack's time in the hospital. Abby and Jack's new dog Happy bounds across the yard, chasing after Jacklyn's dog Buddy. Abby and Jack rented a house with a yard for the dog. It is too soon to know how Buzz's affairs will be sorted out, and I haven't heard if he had a will or who he left his house to. Glancing at my friends who have become family, a smile spreads across my face. Wherever I am with them, it feels like home.

Tex, seated to my left, says, "I'm looking forward to going out on your boat tomorrow on rescue calls."

I nod. Her calm presence reminds me of my mother, who if she had lived would be about the same age. I say, "Be ready for rough weather. They're predicting gale force winds tomorrow afternoon and evening with hazardous conditions. Are you sure you don't want to stay home by the fire instead of going out and bucking waves in howling wind?"

She grins, and her white teeth sparkle. "I'm up for it. Tell me, how did you use the money I gave you? I heard the debt collector and his boss were arrested."

"They were, for tax evasion and money laundering." I glance at Jack, whose brown-eyed gaze catches on mine for a second. Abby is watching us. Craig caused a stir by questioning the legality of their marriage, saying Jack wasn't in his right mind. But his protest fell on deaf ears. Now Jack is able to walk and talk and eat.

I say to Tex in a low voice, "Jack owed money to a lot of people, so we paid off his debts with donations from crowdfunding, selling his sneaker collection and using some of the money you invested."

Abby leans across the table. "I'm sorry there wasn't enough to pay you the missing child support. Ten years is a long time to wait."

I release a long sigh. "It would've been nice."

Abby says, "He wants to get trained as an X-ray or MRI technician and work in a hospital. We'll pay you back, but it'll take a while."

I say, "Thanks. He's a new man after all he's been through."

She says, "He is."

I pat the table for emphasis and say, "You guys make a good couple. I'm going to make a toast, so go stand by Jack."

I wait until Abby is with him, and I stand, raising a red plastic tumbler with iced tea. "Tex, thanks for having us here today. We've been on a journey of heartbreak and healing, and we appreciate you hosting us, so we can put it behind us and start fresh. Now I'd like to raise a toast to the newlyweds. Abby and Jack, may you have many more years of pure joy, smooth sailing and calm seas."

Around the table, people raise glasses and say, "Here, here, to many more years."

Abby's cheeks turn rosy, and she and Jack kiss. He grins and slides his arms around Kelly's and Abby's waists.

I say, "May this be the first of many celebrations with our found family."

We hoist glasses and drink, and I sit down. A soft breeze blows past, caressing my cheeks, and I let out a contented sigh. The course of our lives changed the moment Jack disappeared into the briny Salish Sea. In many ways, life is better, except for Buzz's death. The loss of a dear friend will always tug at our heart strings, but we must carry on.

Tex says, "Have you ever rescued a boat that ran aground?"

"I have." I tell her how I patched a hole in the hull of a trawler-style powerboat and pulled it off a reef in Wasp Passage. She listens with rapt attention.

Laughter erupts from Jacklyn and Mercury, drifting down the table to Kelly, Abby and Jack. I pause in my story and look over the group, take a sip of sweet tea and let the magic of the moment sweep over me. I take a mental snapshot of smiling faces, twinkling lights in over-head tree branches, and the ease of good friends gathered for a meal, and then I finish telling my tale to Tex.

Kelly stands and says, "Shall we play croquet or badminton?"

"Croquet," we all say.

I stand and help Tex clear the table. I don't care if I

win or lose. I'm just grateful Jack is alive, and he is getting along with Kelly.

Outside, I grin and grab a croquet mallet with a blue band for good luck, because it matches the color of the sea today. Kelly steps up to begin the game, shifting her weight from side to side, and she whacks the ball, sending it sailing toward a wicket. I let out a cheer and wish for an easy life for my glorious daughter. We've had enough sadness, regrets and secrets kept. Now it is a time for healing and joy.

65

CRAIG

I overheard at the marina that my friends were spending the day at a rich lady's island estate, but they didn't invite me. I have time on my hands as I await trial. Without Jack's testimony against me, the case is weak, my attorney tells me, but there's a chance he might remember details about the scam, which would send me to prison.

I hop in my boat and cruise through the San Juan Islands west of Millersville. Puttering past Grand Island, I put the engine in idle and pull out my binoculars. Jack should pay for what he did and turning my friends against me. I would've liked to join them and play badminton and drink a beer by the pond or wander on the beach. I could use wealthy backers, like Irena has behind her boat rescue business.

The cooler opens behind me, and a man says, "See them yet?"

I turn to Irena's dad and say, "Yep, got them in my sights."

66

BUZZ

I wake up on the floor wrapped in blankets in a dimly lit cabin. The smell of wood smoke comes from a stone fireplace, where a kettle hangs over a fire. The aroma of some sort of stew wafts past, making my stomach growl with hunger.

A wrinkled, gray-haired old woman missing a front tooth smiles. "You're alive."

My mouth is dry, and I swallow. "Who are you and how did I get here?"

She squats by the fire. "I'll tell you the story, but you might not believe it."

Thank you for reading *By Midnight*! Please let other

readers know what to expect by posting ratings/reviews on Goodreads, Amazon and BookBub.

Next up is **The Winter Storm** My Book

Sign up for my author newsletter on my website to hear about new releases and book deals www.susanspechtoram.com.

Follow me on BookBub for updates

My Facebook author page is: Susan Specht Oram Author

My YouTube channel videos show the setting for my novels (@susanspechtoramauthor).

Thank you for reading my books!

ABOUT THE AUTHOR

Susan is writing mysteries-thrillers with high stakes and heart. Previously, she served as senior director of corporate communications for biotechnology companies. Susan worked as an activity aide in an upscale nursing home's secure psychiatric unit. She was a potter and painter with an art studio in Seattle and has also worked as a market researcher, a nurse's aide, a waitress, and a library page. Her essays have been published in Mothering Magazine, Twins Magazine and Utne Reader.

Susan grew up near Detroit, Michigan and received a BFA with Honors from University of Oregon and a MBA in Marketing from Seattle University. She lives in a windy part of the Pacific Northwest with her husband and their rescue dog.

BOOKS BY SUSAN SPECHT ORAM

Shore Lodge

The Thieves

Cabin Eight

Secrets at the Café

The Mother's Threat

Under Jackson Bridge

Missing Man

By Midnight

The Winter Storm

Humorous fiction:

Boating with Buddy, a report from a canine correspondent

Nonfiction:

Brief business books on investor relations, crisis
communication and public relations

www.ingramcontent.com/pod-product-compliance
Lightning Source LLC
Chambersburg PA
CBHW030141310726
48970CB00005B/1530